STEVEN PAUL WATSON

HOWLING MOON

THE BEGINNING

Livonia, Michigan

HOWLING MOON: THE BEGINNING
Copyright © 2017 Steven Paul Watson

This book is a work of fiction. The characters, incidents, and dialogue are drawn from the author's imagination and are not to be construed as real. Any resemblance to actual events or persons, living or dead, is entirely coincidental.

Published by Umbra
an imprint of BHC Press

Library of Congress Control Number:
2017933757

ISBN-13: 978-1-946006-66-0
ISBN-10: 1-946006-66-1

Visit the publisher at:
www.bhcpress.com

Also available in ebook

With many special thanks to…

My parents, Steve and Etha.
Without you I wouldn't be who I am.

The many beta readers
who have been along for the ride
through the few incarnations
of *Howling Moon*.
You all gave me the support and
confidence to push through
my own self-doubt when I needed it.

To everyone who encouraged me in
this journey to chase my dreams.

And especially my loving wife, Samantha.

And BHC Press
for being so amazing.

I want to thank you all!

For

Bear

HOWLING MOON

MOON

THE BEGINNING

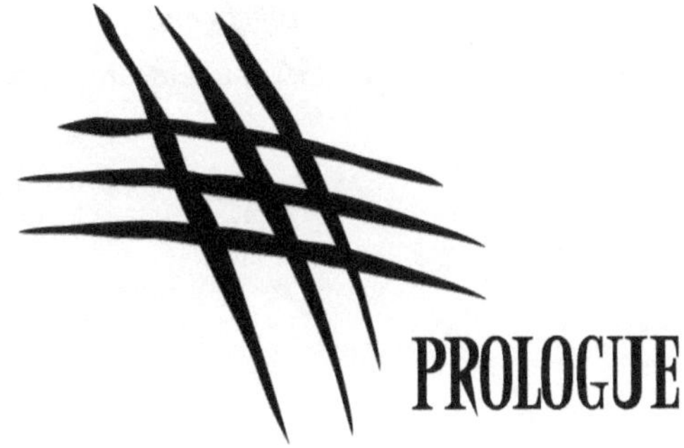

PROLOGUE

SHE RAN. NAVIGATING *the bleak, dreary wilderness with ease, she dodged, jumped, and slid past slashing limbs, broken branches, and deadfalls. Each passing sunrise brought winter nearer and the hunts would prove more difficult. The ground was moist under her feet and soft from days of rain and the hint of snow. The wet and cold made her bones stiff. Still, the taste of fresh blood and flesh on her tongue whet her appetite for the next kill. But this time, she pursued a different prey, one as dangerous as she was. She ached for unhinged violence to quench her blood lust.*

She paused with head lifted high. The forest was silent with the fear of knowing what she was, a predator. The small ones peered down with wide eyes from the safety of the trees. She growled, just for spite and without hesitation, they scattered. She took to the trail made by the strong buck she had tracked for miles, his scent clinging to her nostrils.

She snarled, hearing the deer break through the forest away from her—the creature had yet to learn about the darkness that lingered in the blackest shadows of the world. The smell intoxicated her, and she drank another deep breath, wanting more. It moved, and she rushed to meet it. As it fled, she followed, faster and faster, through the undergrowth. Her heartbeat nearly drowned out the sound of her feet on the ground.

She came to a sudden stop; head in the air, her pursuit of the buck interrupted by a familiar innocent scent. She could already taste her prey as she crept through the undergrowth until a harsh unnatural light blinded her. A young woman's laughter mingled with the breathing of another. She tensed in anticipation, tongue lolling free as she inched forward still cloaked in darkness. There. There was the prey she ached for…

1

West Virginia
October 18

EMILY GLANCED IN the rearview giving herself a reassuring smile as the lights from the gas station grew distant. She took a long deep breath to relax, but the mirror reflected her troubled brown eyes back at her. Her bright-red hair—pulled into a neat ponytail—had lost a few curls and they littered her freckled forehead, damp with perspiration. She could still feel her skin crawl thinking about how the two old men at the gas station had looked at her. She had started to panic when they followed her outside, and she still looked to see if they pursued. Only blackness was nipping at her taillights. It had been years since she'd been on this road and considering the clock said 4:34 a.m., she began to regret her plans to travel home. She'd just wanted to surprise them.

Her favorite radio station had faded thirty minutes ago. Now, only static echoed through the small jeep, the hum of the engine keeping rhythm. It distracted her, momentarily, from the inane pop song stuck in her head. Her high beams lit the blacktop, years past due for new pavement. The highway climbed in curves that hugged the steep mountainside, and she drove with her wheels just inches from the crumbling line on the edge. She felt the drift of each curve, the squeal of rubber yelping out as she took them faster than the vehicle liked. Reaching the top, she accelerated through the dip in the road, her heart skipping a beat and making her smile for real. Misspent adolescence drifted through her mind, times with friends, driving this very road faster than she was going now.

It had been the main route between Ravenswood and Williamson, once upon a time, before I-77 made the drive through the mountain region of the state more accessible. She had only chosen it tonight because of construction on I-77, thinking the old road would allow her to get to her parents' home in Williamson faster. In the short few years, a lot had changed about the place where she had grown up. She hadn't seen it often in that time, living two hours away was a convenient excuse not to return home regularly.

Emily could remember the houses as they used to be, mostly rundown shacks of impoverished families. There were lights on few houses still, but now even they seemed abandoned. Civilization seemed far away in the backwoods of West Virginia. The road sloped down again, and she instinctively let the gas pedal drift free. She hit the seek button on her radio and in a moment the loud crash of drums echoed inside the leather interior. She approached the bottom of the next hill, accelerating despite the yellow danger sign. She knew what came next.

As she came out of the second of the two curves, she glanced back in the mirror, confident she remembered the lay of the road. She grinned again as her heart raced the jeep's engine through the mountain's curves. But when she looked back to the road ahead, something was there. It was there for only a second. With a cold rush of fear and surprise, Emily slammed on the brakes, yanking the vehicle into the other lane. Tires screeched and lost purchase as the car spun off into the wooded darkness.

Emily opened her eyes suddenly to loud drums and an equally harsh-sounding bass voice screaming through the car. As she put her hand to her forehead, she realized the screams came from the radio. She clicked off the noise, but drums continued to pound in her head. The engine still hummed. Her rearview showed only the red glow from her brake lights against the shadowy foliage. She tried the gas gently, and the car slid sideways. Her headlights illuminated an embankment leading up several feet to the road. She gunned the gas this time, and the tires whistled as they spun in the mud from yesterday's rain.

"Shit!" She leaned on the brake. "Shit, shit. Dad is going to love this." She heard a knocking coming from the back of the vehicle. On instinct, she checked her rearview seeing something move away from the rear. She panicked, releasing her foot off the brake, and the jeep slid farther away from safety. She held the brake, securing the vehicle, as she turned, seeing only shadows in the red taillights. "Get it together, Em." She needed to get out of here. She touched the gas again with the same result as before. Sliding the car into park, she sighed, chastising herself more than ever for not getting the one with four-wheel drive. She'd never thought she would need it. She wasn't an off-road kind of girl.

Emily reached for her purse, which had slid across the seat next to her to rest up against the passenger door. She pulled the small bag free and realized her cell phone had been on top of it just before the accident. She unlocked her seat belt and leaned across the seats, but it was nowhere to be seen. She sat up straight with a few choice words her mother would have washed her mouth out for, and then noticed the dim light of her phone on the floor. Finally, a break. As she reached down, her fingers closing around the phone, a loud screech, like nails on a chalkboard startled her motionless. She could feel the vibration as something scratched the driver's side of the vehicle, sending a chill up her back. Staying hunched over, she turned slowly to look out the driver's side window but saw nothing. She sat up straight in her seat trying to control her breathing as she looked out at the darkness beside her.

"Pull it together," she muttered, sliding her thumb across the phone. She sifted through the numbers with a quick glance at the time before she pressed send. The ringing seemed loud in the night, maybe even louder than the engine's hum. Then, a beep. Answering machine. "Hey, Daddy…" she paused, angry with herself. "I know you and Mom told me not to come home for your anniversary but I wanted to surprise you this morning. Breakfast in bed and all of that…" Another long pause. "Um…surprise. I'm stuck out on Old Lake Road…but I'm alright…don't worry." There was a loud clatter as the answering machine cut off. She never expected him to answer at this time of the morning. She knew both of her parents were heavy sleepers. It had been something she took advantage of in her youth sneaking out with friends. The final beep of the answering machine was deafening. She debated calling a second time, but knew it was unlikely to wake them. Emily was partially glad he never answered, twenty-four but she knew he would have acted as if she was sixteen with a learner's permit. She turned the engine off.

Emily reached into the glove box, pulling the small purple flashlight free and quickly clicked the soft button. She shined the light through the windows and checked all around the vehicle before she unlocked the driver's door and pushed it open to the night. As she stepped out, the ground gave under her, the heels of her boots sinking into the mud.

"Perfect," she muttered as the flashlight's tiny glow revealed dark mud covering the top of her black boots. Emily grimaced with frustration and checked out the tires. Thick mud gripped tread and rims alike. She doubted even four-wheel drive would help now. She needed a tow.

Ten miles of hard hiking back to the gas station with the creepy old men was definitely out. There used to be an old bait shop a few miles in the other direction, but she doubted it was open this late. The ranger's station a mile beyond that would be her best bet. There was no way she'd take a ride from anyone out this time of night. She gave an exhausted look at her new boots with their raised heels knowing they were going to be terrible to walk to the ranger's station in. She found herself missing her running shoes, knowing the walk would be brutal on her.

Emily brushed the few loose curls from her eyes. Her head had stopped pounding, but her heart felt as if it was going to escape her chest. The embankment looked climbable if sloppy. She'd been lucky she hadn't hit that cement column. Reaching into the car, she pulled her purse out and dropped her keys inside as she stepped aside and shut the door with a well-placed hip. She made sure the doors were locked and did a final sweep with her flashlight.

Only then did she notice the scratches running the length of the driver's side. A fearful chill raced over her body. The four long scratch marks ran parallel and over an inch apart. And they were deep, down to the metal, the paint peeled up in tiny curls. The hair on the back of her neck stood as she whirled, shining the light into the surrounding woods in a long arc. Maybe she should just wait here it was only a few hours until daybreak. She backed toward the car, sliding in the mud. Her heart began to beat faster as panic built in her stomach. Her hand found the front bumper and followed the comforting steel body of the jeep until she held the cold chrome door handle. She pulled her keys from her purse after a few moments of digging. Her back still pressed to the steel, she fumbled with the keys until she found the buttons. One click and the lights of the jeep blinked, unlocking the doors.

There was a brief moment as she turned and pulled the handle that a warm breeze drifted across her neck. Then something heavy slammed into her. It must have been behind the jeep the entire time, watching her, stalking her. The force knocked her through the brush, several yards away from where she started. She hit the ground hard, her right shoulder at an odd angle. She tried to scramble to safety, but she couldn't place any weight on her right arm, and the mud shifted and slipped under her. In her frantic thrashing, one hand struck tarmac. She had been thrown nearly to the road. She didn't need to look back, to know the thing was still there.

"Help! Help me!" she yelled. Something grabbed her ankle. She dug the fingers of her left hand into the dirt, her right arm still useless, but she wasn't strong enough to resist the creature that pulled her back into the brush.

"No, no, no…"

Intense pain pierced her left side as it bit down through her jacket, shirt and skin, teeth like a hot knife through butter. Emily cried out in pain. Terrified, she frantically tried to roll away, striking blindly at the darkness. The grip on her side released, but the pain intensified. She screamed again, pushing away from the ground with both arms. The pain in her right shoulder was nothing compared to the intense throbbing from her left side. She scrambled on hands and knees, trying to move forward, but only slipping farther down the embankment toward her car. Adrenaline rushed through her, but fear made her feel weak. She knew she was stronger than this. She had run track in high school, but she couldn't find that energy now. She cried out, praying someone would hear her, as she fought for her life.

Emily could hear the creature stirring behind her with unhurried movement as if stalking easy quarry. Her face was soaked with tears, mud and sweat as she finally stumbled to the road. For a brief moment, she tried to run again. A few steps into her sprint, she fell to the rough pavement with a thud jarring her entire body. "Why?" she muttered. She wasn't sure if she even made a sound beyond a whimper.

The pain in her side was excruciating. She ran a hand down her side feeling a sticky wetness on her clothing. She didn't have to see it to know it was blood. Her blood. A shrill scream escaped her lungs.

Emily twisted her body, attempting to locate her attacker, but the darkness kept it hidden. Her right arm hung free, the pain in her shoulder almost nonexistent. Her whole body was numb. "Why?" she asked the darkness. She wasn't sure which way to go as she backed away from the crash site, tripping over her own feet and falling again.

On her back, she looked up at the sky and could see the half-moon as it stared back at her. The clouds had cleared. She could see the stars. A low rumbling growl sounded somewhere behind her.

"Please, God," she mouthed. She tried to roll over onto her stomach but whichever way she went, her body would not accommodate. Finally, she got over onto her right side, curled in a fetal position. She could hear the growl louder now, and closer. It seemed to come from all around her. She squeezed her eyes shut, but she could hear it come nearer. Even felt its breath on her skin. There was nothing she could do but wait for the silence.

EMILY HEARD VOICES *whispering in the darkness. Some were familiar. Some were not. She wanted to call out to them. She wanted to warn them but couldn't remember why. Her heart slowed for a moment, then raced as she imagined hot breath against her neck, saliva dripping down her skin as jaws reached for her again…*

She jolted upright in the bed, staring blankly through her tangled hair that covered her own view. She was surrounded by people who all spoke at once. Someone moved toward her and she recoiled, clinging to the headboard in terror. Her memory was hazy, except the beast. She remembered the animal now. She opened her mouth to explain but instead of words, a chilling scream echoed through the room. She scratched at her left side, her body quaking as she surveyed the strangers around her.

Then someone sat down directly in front of her, their eyes locked. This was not her attacker. She began to see clearer now even with the hair still across her face. She tilted her head to one side.

"Ashley?" The word was barely a whisper and before the young dark-skinned woman could answer, Emily lunged, wrapping her arms around the woman's neck and pulling her close.

Ashley Hayden was her best friend of ten years, and she pulled her tight being sure the other woman was real. Ashley tried to speak through the tight grip, but only a subtle cough escaped. Emily released her as a group of horrified nurses gathered in the doorway. From the looks on their faces, her scream had reached the entire floor. She eyed one, in particular, who sidled closer until she was distracted by Ashley pushing hair from her eyes.

"You're certainly a lucky young woman."

Emily looked at the nurse in the green scrubs again, her eyes a familiar green that demanded attention. She only looked for a moment before looking at the happy faces around the room. She knew all of them.

"How much do you remember?" The nurse took a firm grip on her wrist. The other hand was tight in Ashley's grip.

"Huh…" Emily stared at the nurse, not really understanding.

"How much do you remember?" Ashley repeated the nurse's question.

A look passed between her friend and the nurse.

"Where am I?" Emily turned to look her in the eyes smiling.

"You're in the Charleston Hospital," the nurse replied. "You've been in and out of consciousness for six days. It's the 25th of October."

Emily wasn't really listening. She was counting the streaks of colors in Ashley's hair. Even pulled back into a ponytail, the multiple colors were noticeable, little stripes pulled tightly over her skull. She wore little make-up, a pullover t-shirt with jeans over combat boots, very dressed down and unlike her best friend. It was the details bringing her back, this wasn't a dream. The nightmare was over.

"You look like hell," Emily said, looking away from the other woman's dark brown eyes. Everyone in the room looked pale to her. She could almost hear their hearts racing. Their stares made her skin crawl and stomach churn. Emily was using her friend's streaked hair as a distraction. Focusing on the streaks, she tried to avoid the question.

"Me? You ought to look in the mirror, darling," Ashley retorted. The grip on her friend's hand grew tighter. "Now, what do you remember?"

Emily smiled as she looked away. Her parents were dressed very casually, too. They looked like they hadn't slept in days. Her dad's arm wrapped tightly around her mom's shoulders.

"What's wrong with her?" her mother questioned. Emily glanced at her mom who looked at the nurse. Emily followed her mother's gaze to the green-eyed nurse who stared at the moment and then to Emily.

"She's in shock." The nurse tried to take Emily by her wrist, and she jerked away. There was a familiarity about the nurse she couldn't explain. The woman's hair was pulled back in a ponytail exposing her flawless face, but Emily could see the frustration in her expression grew. It was in her eyes as they grew a darker green. "The doctor will be along shortly." The nurse stomped off, giving a last fleeting glance back before disappearing out of sight.

"I remember"–there was a distinct pause, as she pulled her hands away from her friend, reaching to her left– "the accident." She placed her hand against the wound, causing an instant grimace from the pain. She looked up at Ashley. "An animal… I thought I was dead."

"What kind of animal?"

She turned, seeing a young man on the opposite side of the bed from the others. She remembered him and smiled. Her eyes locked on Colin Forsyth, an old friend with shoulder-length, shaggy, dirt-blond hair, scruffy face and big teeth-filled grin. He wore a pullover long-sleeve shirt with khaki pants of matching tan colors. The clothes looked big on his thin frame, his hands hidden in his pockets as he looked down at her.

"I never saw it clearly," she replied. It was not a complete lie, but each time she blinked, she remembered the flash of shadow in her rear-view mirror. The angry yellow eyes that looked into her for a moment were full of hunger. "Last thing I remember…" she paused again.

Silence reigned, as even the monitors seemed to wait for more of her story. She watched her mother move to stand beside Ashley at the edge of the bed.

"I was in the road…laying there in the road. And I could feel it sitting on top of me. It was…big. It was like everywhere at once but nowhere. It struck out of the darkness." Emily wrapped her arms around her chest tightly, feeling every moment of that night coming back to her now. Every step she took, every heartbeat—when she tried to run but got nowhere. "How did I get to the hospital?"

"An old man happened by and almost hit you he said. But any animal was long gone." Ashley reached her hand out and placed it on Emily's arm.

Emily shivered. Ashley's hand felt like ice against her too-warm skin.

"You should rest now," Ashley said, pulling her hand away.

Emily said nothing but smiled.

"We're glad you're okay," chimed in Colin before exiting the room.

"Get some rest, sweetie," Mom said, leaving right after the young man.

"I told you not to come home," Dad said. He looked down at his daughter with his typical demanding smile and frustrated eyes. She remembered the disappointed stare well from her days in high school.

"I just wanted to surprise you." She gave him a weak smile that he returned, even if he didn't mean it.

"Get your rest. We'll talk about this later."

Emily watched until her dad was gone before she turned back to the only person left in the room.

"He was out looking for you, you know," Ashley said, "when he got the call you were brought here. I haven't heard him say more than two words since I got here."

Emily lay back on the bed and Ashley tucked the covers up around her. In a moment, she drifted off to sleep.

———————◆———————

SHE WOKE MORE peacefully this time, slowly lifting herself up from the bed while looking around the room. She saw the plate of covered food on the table. She had been asleep when Colin returned. "How long was I out?"

"Six hours," Ashley replied after looking at her watch. She sat in a chair at the side of the bed with a small blanket covering the lower part of her body. "I made everyone else go home and get some sleep."

"When is the last time you slept?" Emily rolled to her right side, keeping an eye on her friend. For a moment, nothing hurt. She had forgotten about her right shoulder.

"Last night."

"In a bed?" Emily questioned with a coy smile.

"Seven days ago. You'd be surprised. These chairs are quite comfortable," she lied.

"How bad is it?" Emily braced herself. It had been in all of their eyes, from the nurse to the doctors. She could see it more clearly in Ashley's eyes and the rumble of her throat biting on words.

"Your wounds? The doctor said you should make a full recovery. They have you on antibiotics for any infections. Shot you up with some concoction in case you have rabies. I told them there was no need. It's not like anyone would be able to tell a difference if you started going crazy and foaming at the mouth." A mischievous smile spread across Ashley's face. Her friend shifted her weight out of the chair onto her feet on the floor.

Emily chuckled but she stopped when pain shot up her side.

"There were other attacks on the same road," Ashley added.

"Survivors?"

Ashley just shook her head.

"How many?"

"Four dead."

Emily felt a chill run across her entire body. "Do they know what it was?"

"There have been a couple detectives here and wildlife officials. First, they thought it was a wolf by the bites and claw marks, but I overheard the female enforcement officer talking about it being too big for a wolf. They thought maybe a bear or an exotic animal, someone's pet lion or something."

Emily smiled wider than she should have.

"What's so funny?"

"This lady cop…was she cute?"

"I never noticed," Ashley replied archly, ignoring Emily's smile.

"Uh-huh. I'm on my deathbed and you're looking to get your flirt on."

"I did not…" Ashley huffed. "And besides, you're not dying." She turned her attention back to the phone in her hand.

"How close was it?" Emily counted the ceiling tiles.

"Too close." Ashley put a cool hand on her friend's arm, squeezing tightly. "But you're okay now. The worst is behind you."

Emily's free hand drifted to her left side and the tender flesh hidden under the gown and thick bandages.

"It can't hurt you now. I won't let it."

Emily was so grateful for friends like Ashley, and the whole thing seemed a distant nightmare. Maybe Ash was right. The worst was behind her.

———●———

SHE REACHED OUT through the darkness, grasping at nothing but air. Air and the something breathing. "Hello?" Her voice cracked, her throat ached, and her heart pounded as she waited for a reply. Nothing. "Who's there?" It was then she felt the familiar breath on her neck. Warm and wet breath on her bare skin, making every hair stand. Oh, so slowly she turned, looking, trying to avoid notice. But there was nothing there, except those yellow eyes.

Emily jerked from sleep, half off the bed. She raised her head and looked around before letting her head hit the pillow. It was soaked with sweat. Her hand brushed loose curls from the cold wetness of her forehead.

"Nightmares?"

Emily quickly looked up.

In the doorway was a woman, standing with one hand on the frame and the other on her hip. She had long, straight, dark hair pulled tightly back without a strand out of place. A black pinstriped suit top with matching skirt and red lips set off the woman's pale complexion. Complete with matching jet-black, six-inch heels, she looked professional from head to toe.

"Who are you?"

"Illyania Knox," the woman said, taking a couple steps into the room. She looked around quickly as if to assure herself they were alone.

"You're Dad's friend, right?" The other woman nodded. "A psychiatrist…"

"Have the nightmares started?" the woman asked as she walked around the bed. She didn't look at Emily but sat in the chair beside the bed.

"I don't need a psychiatrist," Emily said quickly.

Knox smiled largely and leaned back in the chair. "You nearly died in an accident."

"I was attacked by a wild animal. It was not an accident." Emily rolled away from Knox, hoping she'd get the hint and leave. She tried to keep her weight off the wound with her shoulder and legs, but anytime the mattress touched her side, the pain intensified. She bit her lip, refusing to make a sound, but she couldn't stop the tears that came with each throbbing heartbeat.

"Fine. You survived a 'traumatic' experience. Your father thought you might need to talk to someone."

"She has someone." A familiar voice broke the tension. Emily could have kissed Ashley, standing in the door, hands on hips and a mean stare just for Knox.

"It's always nice to have someone to talk to" Knox reached into the pocket of her suit jacket and pulled out a card. She carefully placed it on the stand beside the bed. "But sometimes it is better to seek an outside ear."

Ashley watched every move the older woman made crossing the room until she made her exit. She quickly shut the door and turned back to Emily. Emily rolled to her back with a sigh of relief and threw her forearm across her tear-filled eyes.

"Bitch," Ashley muttered loudly, taking her usual seat in the chair.

"I just want to go home," Emily whined, her eyes still covered by her arm.

"I heard the doctor tell your dad you may be released tomorrow," Ashley replied, picking up the card and crumpling it up before tossing it into the garbage basket.

Emily closed her eyes for a moment taking a deep breath. "How mad is he?"

"Your dad? On a level of is he more worried or irrationally mad because you wanted to come home and surprise your parents even though he told you not to?"

Emily opened her eyes looking at her friend, her eyes focused on hers.

"He's your dad. You can't expect rational. Even when it comes to you."

There came a soft knock at the door. A doctor and two nurses stepped inside. "How are you doing Ms. Meyer?" The doctor looked no older than her. He had a charming big smile.

"You tell me?" she questioned.

"You're a very lucky young lady," he replied approaching.

She could tell he was older than she had initially thought. The nurse who approached her first was the same one with the deep-green eyes.

"I'm Doctor Evans. I just wanted to check in on you. How is your pain level?"

Emily looked at the nurse as she circled around to the other side. Ashley reached over grabbing hold of her hand.

"I don't really feel it," she lied. "When can I go home?" She rushed her question, watching the nurse pull and tug at the gown until the wound on her side was exposed.

"We're waiting on some blood work before we can clear you."

"But she will get out of here soon?" Ashley questioned. Emily squeezed her friend's hand tighter.

"We will see." His smile was more than just charming, it was gorgeous. She watched him as he inspected the wound. "I need to know if you feel any discomfort."

 felt his cold hands on her side sending a chill up her body. The pain was there, but it was manageable. She closed her eyes taking a deep breath.

"Your hands are cold," she muttered through gritted teeth. She could hear his snicker as she took another deep breath. Her senses were on fire. She could smell the mesh of cologne and perfume, covering the smell of sex. She opened her eyes looking at the other nurse at the back of the room. The nurse watched Doctor Evans's every move and Emily smiled.

"Sorry," Doctor Evans replied. "The color looks good. There is still some bruising. We'll see how the blood work looks and we may get you out of here soon."

Emily watched the doctor and the nurses leave the room.

"Are you hungry?" Ashley questioned.

"I think I'm going to get some sleep," Emily replied, lying back into the pillow.

EMILY WOKE. THE room was mostly dark, though some light came in through the door out into the hall. She looked over to where she expected to see Ashley. The chair was pulled back into the corner.

"I sent her back to your home, to get you some clothes."

She didn't have to look to know her own father's voice.

"They're releasing me?" Emily quickly questioned, turning to look at her father. He sat across the room against the back wall.

"First thing in the morning."

Emily smiled. "I'm sorry."

"For what?"

She could hear the anger in his voice. It was only two words, but she knew the tone. "Never mind." She closed her eyes. "I should have listened."

"I'm glad you're okay."

She opened her eyes hearing him stand up. The creak of the hospital chair was deafening. She felt the bed shift and then his hand on her forehead as she opened her eyes.

"You should not have been out that time of the night."

"I know."

"The road was wet, it's in bad shape, and you haven't had to come that way in years."

"I know." She closed her eyes hoping it would be the end of the conversation.

"It could have been worse."

She felt his hand leave her. Only a moment later, he left the room.

"I know."

3

October 27

EMILY STEPPED OUT through the door. Her vision was foggy, and she had a hard time making out her surroundings. The only thing that made sense was the moon. The center field out in front of her was easy to see, except a thin fog as it hung around waist high.

"Hello?" She was confused. The last thing she remembered was the drive to her parents' house. "Anyone there? Mom…Dad?"

She took a few steps forward. She glared at her feet, the boots covered in fresh mud as they covered the black leggings. This wasn't what she was wearing when she left for her parents'. The loose-fitting flannel shirt, half-unbuttoned was also not her style. She'd not noticed the cold air until she felt she was exposed to anyone who may be watching.

She turned looking back at the cabin. It was familiar to her, but it didn't come to her at first as she turned looking back over the field. It was her grandmother's place. She heard a dog bark, off in the distance, causing her heart to race.

"Aries?" She stepped forward into the darkness. "Come here, boy." She smiled. Again, a dog barked off in the distance. "Aries?" She rushed farther out into the field, and the fog grew thicker around her. She finished buttoning the shirt up close to her throat. She felt the shooting pain run up her side and it took her breath away as she leaned forward. She coughed feeling the pain in her side. It was coming back now…she'd never made it to her parents' home.

She heard the rumbling of something running behind her. She quickly turned seeing nothing. "Aries…" She could hear the growling now, it was nothing like she had heard from her old dog. And it came back to her now—the feeling of despair when Aries died shortly after her eighteenth birthday. She again heard the rumbling behind her as she turned quickly. She could see the eyes now—the same eyes from the night of the accident as the large figure lunged through the darkness with an eerie howl.

Emily jerked up from her sleep, her forehead covered in sweat. The heart monitor at her side was going erratic.

"I'm sorry…I didn't mean to wake you."

A man was sitting a vase of flowers on the small table just inside the room.

Emily struggled to catch her breath. There was no one else in the room.

"Looks like you were having a very intense nightmare." The man smiled as he messed with the flowers. His smile was abnormal in the dim light of the room. His teeth seemed to glow as his face disappeared and there was only the smile.

"Do you…" Emily looked around the room, her hand on the bed's nurse call button. "Do you work here?"

"I'm sorry. I work for a florist, just watering flowers, Ms. Meyer." The man again smiled before leaving the room.

Emily lay back trying to catch her breath, but she could still remember the dream. Though it was more than that, she was remembering the nightmare of the night of the attack. She closed her eyes. It was over now. She was safe.

———————————●———————————

EMILY PRESSED HER weight against the door, there was barely enough room in the bathroom for her but Ashley insisted. Her friend sat on the closed toilet handing her clothes. Emily pulled the jeans up latching the brown belt about her hips. She faced away from the mirror through the process of undressing and redressing until all that remained was buttoning the long-sleeve black shirt. She turned facing her reflection, taking a deep breath before looking down her body, past the white bra, ignoring all the small scrapes and bruises. It was not easy to ignore, she was covered in small bruises and scratches. She had seen the scar on her ankle, even the long gash marks on her right arm, but none of those wounds hurt like her left side. She looked at the tender flesh, the purple bruising with stitches sewn to flesh where she had been bitten. She had pulled the bandage free despite orders to leave it dressed, staring in disbelief, the scars made it real. It was not just a vivid nightmare.

"Did you ask the doctor?"

Emily looked back. "Huh?"

"Will it scar?"

"He said it would mostly heal, all but this. It will leave a scar, but he tried to reassure me it would not be noticeable." She bit her lip, peering at her friend.

Ashley looked different from the day before, more like the friend she had grown to love. Ripped jeans with knee-high black boots, two black belts lay upon her hips with no purpose other than she enjoyed wearing them. A bust-revealing white tank top covered with a black vest left little to the imagination. She liked her push-up bras making her small breasts more noticeable, and a rope necklace disappeared into her cleavage drawing even more eyes to her bust.

"Why are you smiling?"

"I'm just glad you're okay."

She watched her smile. Her purple-tinted lipstick and eyeliner set off her blue contact lenses and lit her tanned skin.

Emily quickly applied the bandage and buttoned up her shirt.

"I know what you need."

Emily knew the grin and shook her head. "I need a night's sleep in my own bed." She turned, opening the door to the room. Her mom was sitting in the chair beside the door. "Where's Dad?"

"He had an appointment he couldn't postpone."

Emily frowned. She wanted to talk to him about the night before but was also glad he was absent. "Has the nurse come by yet?"

"They said they would be back with a wheelchair."

Emily dropped her head back on her shoulders looking at the ceiling. "I don't need a wheelchair. I just want to go home."

"You know honey; you could stay with us for a few days."

Emily forced a smile looking at her mom. Edna Meyer was only in her early fifties and still looked young. Emily knew she had become more comfortable with aging as she had stopped incessantly dying her hair trying to make her normal red that she had lost in her thirties. Emily looked at her with worry, the same worry she saw reflected back in her brown eyes. She looked as if she aged a decade in just a few days.

"Are you okay?" Emily asked.

"Fine. I'm just worried about you."

"It is behind me now." Emily smiled ignoring the invitation from her mom as the nurse entered with the wheelchair.

———————◆———————

IT WAS AN hour drive in peak traffic before they reached Emily's home in Ravenswood. Summer Lane was filled with Bungalow styled homes—all stacked side-by-side neatly together with small yards, drives and neatly maintained roads. Mostly twenty-something's, fresh out of college and beginning their careers, lived in the neighborhood. Emily rested her head against the window until they pulled into the drive. She hesitated to get out of the car, watching Ashley circle around the front to her side.

"I'm not carrying you inside."

Emily sat up opening the door, she stepped out taking a close look around the neighborhood, she could hear a dog barking off somewhere down the street. She could smell people barbecuing—possibly for the last time before winter—and she sighed smelling fresh food.

"Besides I have wine waiting inside."

"I can't have any with these drugs." Emily shook the bag of pill bottles with frustrating force.

"I never said any of it was for you."

Emily circled to the front of the one-story home. Like all others on her street, it was white vinyl, black shingled roof with a small sheltered porch out front. The yard was plain with the exception of a small unattended flowerbed near the walk to the front door.

"Are you coming?"

Emily's stomach growled. She looked to the door not realizing Ashley was waiting for her.

The light was already on when Emily entered, the room was a modest living space, two small red couches, and a chair surrounding a small red oak table. A number of worn fashion magazines and notebooks scattered on the top of the handcrafted table. The walls were a pale tan long past a need of a fresh coat. A thirty-two-inch television hung in the corner thick with dust on the screen, underneath a small cabinet with two plants sat in their pots in need of watering. The floors were a cherry hardwood throughout the entrance only hidden in spots by throw rugs under the couches and just inside the door of the home both of a light red coloring. The walls of the entrance were plain with the exception of three photos, one of Emily and her parents on graduation day, and another of Colin, Ashley, and Emily on the same day. The third was of Ashley and Emily—older versions of them from the previous two photos—both looking under the weather from a long night. Space was clean from where a fourth once hung.

Ashley tossed her leather jacket on the nearest couch and turned to look at her friend. "Food? My treat."

Emily smiled.

"I heard your stomach growling on the drive, but I didn't think you would want some greasy fast food. I know how you are about that stuff."

"Thank you." Emily quickly excused herself, entering the only bedroom. A large king size bed—too big for the small room—split the room in half with its large black comforter and ten pillows of a variety of sizes and colors.

"You made my bed," Emily said out loud but heard no reply from Ashley in the other room. She had remembered leaving it in a mess the night she left. The hall where she entered held a small dresser worn with age, scratched, and marked up where once stickers clung to the dark surface. Beside the dresser were still open folding doors to a walk-in closet with shoes and boots scattered on the floor. A long steel rod held the weight of her clothes—business attire for her job as a lawyer's clerk on the left, jeans and another assortment of pants and skirts hung in the middle, while the right was all shirts and jackets—clothing she wore out on the few occasions she got to go out and have a drink with Ashley. Most all were sectioned off by colors and season in their respective places. She crossed to the opposite side of the room where a small cabinet sat with pictures from her youth until present day sat scattered with other folders and documents. A track trophy sat in the corner. It was the one time she had come in first place in high school. A doorway into a master bathroom crept open as she approached. She stepped in setting the small bag of medicine on the counter beside the assortment of scattered make-up.

Emily looked at the mirror. Her curly red hair fell about her face and hid her shoulders and a lot of the freckles. Her lips were rough and chapped. Her eyes were red and puffy from crying with black underlying circles from exhaustion.

"You made it," she mumbled, half expecting a reply from her reflection. She could hear music. Light and instrumental dark violins covered the sound of the whistle from the heating coming from the vents. She took a deep breath, unbuttoned her long-sleeve shirt, and tossed it to the hamper in the corner. She twisted to one side slowly pulling the bandage free to get a closer look at the bite mark on her waist. With each touch, she felt a shock of pain run up her body like needles being pushed deep into her flesh. The searing pain still did not stop her from touching the purple flesh around the wound. There were moments when she closed her eyes that she could still feel the beast's jaws clamped down on her waist. She was sure she screamed when it happened.

Emily looked to the stitches only imagining what the wound looked like fresh. The impressions from the animal's jaws were visible where sharp canines tore flesh and Doctor Evans had expressed how lucky she was no damage was done internally.

She finished pulling the bandage free, despite some pain from the tape, and tossed it into the garbage by the sink. She reached for the simple white t-shirt sitting on the nearby towel rack and pulled it over her head before dragging her hair free. The shirt was two sizes too big for her and worn out from time and wear. It left much of her shoulder exposed. She shifted seeing the stitches on her shoulder where the beast had first attacked her. It was more bruised than cut.

Emily glanced at the countertop for a minute before she rushed back through the house. Ashley was in the kitchen with a glass of wine in hand when Emily got to the counter grabbing the keys in one swift motion.

"What are you doing?"

Emily unlocked the door stepping out into the garage; the flicker of the overhead lights took a moment before lighting up the garage and her jeep.

Emily knew her dad had arranged for her vehicle to be hauled home after the accident. She walked across the nearly empty garage kneeling down at the driver's side door. She felt Ashley lingering over her shoulder a moment later.

"You see this?" Emily glanced back at her friend seeing her expression go from curiosity to shock as she leaned down beside her.

"What kind of animal could do that?"

Emily placed her hand on the door where four rigid cuts of something sharp had shaved across the door. "The *animal* that attacked me did this! It was toying with me. The moment I crashed it saw me as nothing more than a meal and it could have killed me any fucking time it wanted to!"

Emily felt her friend's head lean into her shoulder. She could feel Ashley's heartbeat they were so close. "I can't..." She heard her say but nothing more came out. Emily allowed her own head to fall onto her friend's. She knew there were no words that could help her—either of them.

"Come, let's get some food maybe you will feel better."

———————◆———————

EMILY SAT STARING at the tea in her hand, a blanket draped across her lower body. "That is your fifth glass of wine." Emily gave Ashley a wicked glare from the opposite couch.

"I'm not going anywhere."

"You don't have to do that," Emily quipped.

"You think you can stop me?"

Emily gritted her teeth watching Ashley take another drink. She could see the amusement in her friend's eyes.

"A couple nights, Em, make sure you are well enough to care for yourself before we go back to living all alone."

"I'll be fine."

"I know you will, but would you rather it was me or one of your parents here sleeping on the couch? I'm sure your father would love to invite Doctor Knox over to shrink your head."

"He was just worried about me."

"Maybe, but it was too soon. He could have waited until after you were released."

There was a pause as they stared at each other over their drinks before Emily spoke. "Do you think I should see her?"

"Your choice and no one else should make it for you," Ashley stated raising her glass for a toast and quickly swallowing down the last of her drink. "I believe I'm going to take a shower. Have you taken your medicine?"

"No, Mother," Emily replied. She watched her friend as she circled the coffee table, their eyes glued on one another until Ashley disappeared behind the couch. Only a moment passed before she felt the other woman's head press on the back of her own.

"I'm glad you're okay."

Emily breathed a sigh of relief hearing her best friend walk away. She waited until she heard the door shut before she uncovered her body lifting the t-shirt up to look at her side. She bit her lip looking at the wound and was sure it looked worse than before. "Not sure I am."

She whimpered as she stood. Each step she took through the house her side seemed to hurt, she stopped at the bathroom sink. She struggled with the lid, a curse on her lips before it finally broke free. She spread the three pills on the counter, two of one and a solo third. She took the biggest putting it in her mouth just before she splashed water from the sink to drink it down. Followed closely by the remaining two forcing them down with another drink, her throat was raw and it hurt just to breathe.

She looked up at herself in the mirror, the water still pouring into the sink. Her brown eyes were bloodshot as she fought tears. She was sure she could hear Ashley in the other bathroom crying. "You're going to be alright," she pronounced trying to convince her reflection. She splashed water onto her face clearing the sweat away and then drank another sip of water before she turned the faucet off. She turned the light off leaving the room and heading for the bed and its thick covers, hoping for a dreamless night.

EMILY SAT UP in bed. Everything was bleak except the light shining through the thin olive curtains. They floated into the room dancing between darkness and light. She pushed her covers free instantly feeling goose bumps from the cracked window. Crossing the room with her arms against her chest, she quickly shut the window and felt the warmth from the nearby vent instantly. Opening the curtains she realized the light stalking in through the window was from a full moon and not the streetlights. She spied the oval orb high in the sky and placed her right hand on her wounded side.

Emily let the curtains fall and walked out to the living room. The cold air stopped her in her tracks. The couch where she left Ashley the night before was abandoned all but a rumpled blanket. She held her arms tight against her rushing to the open front door.

"Ash? Ashley?" Emily turned back inside grabbing a nearby blanket and wrapping it tightly around her own shoulders. She stepped out into the moonlight with bare feet on rough cobblestone walk, her eyes drawn to the clear starless sky.

Emily turned looking back at the door. "Where are you?" She bit her lower lip looking around at the well-lit neighborhood. She felt like something was watching her. Panic set in as she rushed back into the house, slamming the door behind her.

Emily rushed to the guest bathroom expecting to find it locked but the door crept open at the touch of her hand and only darkness greeted her. She flipped the light on followed by the crack of a bulb blowing; Emily jumped back several steps before she realized what happened. She pulled the blanket tighter crossing to the front window and peeking out to see her friend's car; she hadn't even looked a moment before, so distracted by the moon.

"Ashley this isn't funny." She tried to sound mad but she was beginning to shake. A tear slid down her cheek. She rushed to the kitchen and then out into the garage but still no Ashley.

Back into the living room, her breathing was becoming heavier and faster as her eyes locked on her friend's phone on the table. "Ashley," she screamed. She was no longer trying to stay calm.

Emily rushed into the bedroom to her bed, grabbing the jeans from the edge and quickly pulling them on. Boots over bare feet and then a large sweatshirt over the old t-shirt. She opened the drawer of the nightstand pulling out the large flashlight, grabbed her cell phone from the top of the dresser, and started out of the room.

A light whispered moan from the master bathroom stopped her in her tracks. Emily froze slowly turning to look back at the open door. "Ashley?" she questioned but it came out as a whisper. She could see only darkness. She took a couple of steps forward and stared into the light deprived room. It wasn't until she reached the edge of the bed that she remembered she held a tight grip on the flashlight. A click of the button shined a light into the room and reflected it off the tiled walls and floor. She could see nothing.

She slowly walked to the room turning on the light without stepping inside. A couple steps farther she looked to the mirror and could see her eyes puffy and red from tears. Emily turned away from the mirror falling to the floor pushing away from the large tub. "Ashley!" she screamed.

Her friend lay in the corner of the tub, her head over to one side. Emily could see her throat from her position on the floor. Ripped open, the blood was black and steam billowed from the wound making a slight gargle when it met cold air. Her head held in place only by strands of cartilage, skin, and bone—eyes open with a blank stare, her hair matted with the blood. Emily mumbled incoherently. It was hard for her to breathe, as if her chest was collapsing in on itself. She quickly dialed 911 but heard only a beep of no signal. She slowly lifted up onto her knees crawling over to the bathtub. She leaned against the tub and slowly turned Ashley's head toward her pushing the wet hair from her eyes. She could hardly see for the tears now. Her hand shook feverishly. She had a hard time pushing the hair from the other woman's eyes. Ashley was still in the same clothing she remembered her wearing before her shower, her white tank top and cleavage soaked in blood.

Emily sat back in her corner attempting to dial 911 again. Again, no service. She raced to her feet and into the bedroom picking up the cordless landline. Only a busy signal waited her efforts just like before. A cool breeze engulfed her; the fresh taste of outside air on her tongue forced her to rush to the doorway. Her entire body trembled in terror. The door to the outside was open again allowing the moonlight to march in. She turned quickly shutting the door to the bedroom before slowly sitting with her back to it. A loud crash came from the living room and then a harsh thump against the door. The force knocked her forward onto her stomach. She quickly turned, sitting up, and scurried on her hands away from it just as another thunderous crash came against the door. She saw it shake as the plaster on the wall around the door crumbled from the force. She did not stop moving until she was inside the bathroom, quickly shutting and locking the door behind her. She positioned herself on the opposite wall.

Her tears had stopped and she wheezed with every heavy breath. She looked at Ashley with her eyes still open as if to stare at her in a questioning "why?"

The sound of the beast crashing through the door in the other room and the impact on the bathroom door seemed to happen instantaneously.

"Go away!" Emily's voice cracked. Her wounds from the other attack all ached as tears streamed down her face. There was a pause in the attacks on the door. Emily heard nothing from the other room. She slowly stood trying not to look at the bathtub. One step, then a second and she heard it on the other side of the door—sniffing trying to get its prey's scent. She took a step backward looking toward her friend. She wanted to call to her, yell at her saying she promised not to let it get to her again. Instead she grabbed the curtain hiding the body behind it.

She could still hear it as she opened the top drawer of the cabinet. She found nothing she could use as a weapon. She carefully shut each drawer as quietly as she could after sifting through old make-up containers and cleaning products. She paused at the last drawer and looked to the countertop, the aerosol container sat beside several others. With one swift motion, Emily grabbed it, and opened the top left drawer once again pulling out a long-stem lighter. She turned clicking on the lighter several times before she had a steady flame. She dropped to her knees still hearing the animal on the other side. She placed the flame as close to the bottom of the door as she dared with the can of hair spray not far behind.

The long flame escaped under the opening as she touched the trigger on the spray. Two more times she allowed flames to escape but now heard nothing from the other side.

Emily dropped to the floor looking underneath to the small opening. She could see nothing from the other room. She took a deep breath. A thunderous crash, the top of the door cracked and splintered, followed by intense growls of anger from the other side.

Emily moved to the back of the room again with her knees pulled tight against her chest. "Please, God," she whimpered. She glanced to the bathtub through the thin curtain to her friend, just as the door crashed in.

"EMILY."

She heard her voice. She sat up in her bed nearly pushing the other woman off to the floor. Ashley's face filled with shock and horror and immediately Emily realized it was a horrible nightmare. Emily clasped her hands over her face crying, it was only a moment later she felt the other woman pulling her closer into her chest.

"Hey, hey…it was only a dream."

Emily pushed Ashley away from her, far enough until she could look at her neck. She reached her hand out letting her fingers run down her throat, she could feel her friends pulse racing.

"What is it?"

Emily could still see the blood from her dream. "A nightmare," Emily muttered. She let herself fall back to the bed looking at the clock to see it still was not midnight.

"Do you want to talk about it?"

"It seemed so real."

"It sounded real too. You might have woke the neighbors with your screams."

Emily sat up quickly rushing from the room, she could hear Ashley only a couple steps behind. She reached the front door looking through the peephole for a moment before she opened it walking out into the darkness. The sky was cloudy, the moon hidden in the darkness. She turned looking at Ashley in the doorway, "That was too real, Ash."

"Talk to me."

Emily turned looking back into the darkness, the nights air was cold but a chill ran up her back feeling like she was being watched. "Okay." She walked back to the door. She did not stop until they were back inside and she had secured every lock on the door. With her back to the door, she found herself again staring at Ashley's throat.

"Why do you keep staring at my neck?"

"You were in my nightmare."

Ashley's complexion went ghostly. Emily walked past her grabbing her by the wrist and pulling her forcefully to the couch where she told her about her dream.

5

THE BEDROOM ALARM raged at Emily, waking her. Her head nestled on a pillow perfectly positioned in Ashley's lap. When she fidgeted, stretching her legs, Emily pretended to still be asleep not wanting to leave the comfort of Ashley's side. She barely remembered falling asleep with the help of several large glasses of wine. Ashley's fingers ran through her hair triggering her to tremble at the unexpected touch.

"Morning," Ashley murmured, her hand on Emily's forehead. "You've cooled off since last night."

Emily rolled over, noting Ashley's worried face. "I'm fine, Ash," she reassured her. Ashley didn't look convinced. She tried distraction. "So, what's on the schedule for today, Mother?"

"Once you get off me, I'm going to crawl under those beautiful covers on your bed and sleep."

Emily smiled as Ashley's petite fingers roamed through her hair. It was funny to her how the simplest touch from her friend made her feel safe.

"I don't want to move." Emily tugged the blanket tighter, still smiling.

"Then I think," Ashley grumbled playfully before she smiled, "I may have to put you back in the hospital. You've put my legs to sleep. I can't even feel my toes. I may have to forcefully move you." Ashley stuck her tongue out at her friend.

Emily relented, her friend was obviously exhausted. She sat up and leaned her head on the other woman's shoulder. "You have the sweetest pillow talk."

"And you have dragon's breath," Ashley replied, her head drifting closer to Emily. A ringing phone broke the moment.

Emily slowly stood reaching her feet in a stretch, her entire body creaked and ached. She crossed to the kitchen counter to answer it.

"Hello?" She frowned examining the caller id. "It's dad," she explained.

Ashley flashed a sympathetic smile and headed for the back bedroom.

Emily sighed not wanting to answer but knew if she didn't it would be a constant headache throughout the morning until she did answer his call. She placed the phone to her ear after answering, "Hey Dad." She was prepared for the long list of questions. She knew why he was calling and she could picture him sitting there with his doctor's notepad with all the clinical questions ready to check each off as he asks them.

"Hey sweetheart," said a fatherly voice, she could tell he had been awake for a while. His tone always cold and straightforward with her. Even as a child, he'd often talked to her more like she was a patient than his own kid. "Just calling to check in."

"I'm fine. Glad to be home."

"Did you sleep?"

"I got some."

"Ashley taking care of you?"

Question two. She wondered just how many he had to ask before she could confidently bail on the phone call without him calling back with more.

"Of course she is." She wanted to groan but tried to keep her voice calm and direct.

"Emily…" He paused. "There's a card for Dr. Knox in the glove compartment of your jeep. I know you may not want to hear this but, after what happened, it would be good for you to talk with someone…professional."

"I'll think about it," she hedged. Emily didn't want to say anymore. Given the history between her father and Knox, she wondered what Mom would say if she knew he was pushing this. She just wanted the conversation to end, so she could crawl back under the covers and go to sleep. She was sure Ashley would let her crawl into her own bed and sleep the day away.

"That's all I am asking," he replied.

It was easy for her to tell he wasn't happy, because his voice became hoarse. She could remember how he liked to berate and complain when she was younger in the same tone.

"Well, I will let you get breakfast." There was an awkward silence. Then, "I love you."

"Love you, too," she said, turning the phone off before setting it back on the counter.

———————◆———————

BY THE TIME the sun emerged from the morning fog, Emily found herself outside in her favorite lounge chair on the porch—a silly fairy-tale romance in hand. The wind was cold, but she was bundled in a small copper-colored jacket pulled tight around her. A half-filled cup of cold coffee sat on the small metal table at her side. It was her third cup already, even though one was her limit most days. She looked up from her book at the sound of a vehicle and wasn't too surprised to see the Wildlife Enforcement jeep.

Two officers exited the jeep and approached her. The leader was a thin older man in his late fifties with dusty brown hair just starting to thin on top. His eyes hid behind dark sunglasses as he chewed gum. Emily imagined she smelled Nicorette and smoke in waves, over and over with each clench of his jaw and puff of air. He walked up the cobblestone footpath, reaching her first.

"Miss Meyer? Miss Emily Meyer?" His voice was rough with authority, as he swept his sunglasses away from sharp blue eyes. "I'm Henry Williams and this is Vanessa Myra."

Emily set the book on the table, careful not to lose her page. "What can I do for you?" Emily squinted looking up into the sun at them. She began to panic, trying to take a deep breath but couldn't do anything more than whimper.

"We're with the West Virginia Wildlife Enforcement Office," his partner chimed in. She was shorter but not by much with her hair pulled back from her face in a ponytail revealing a dark flawless complexion, plump full lips, and sharp eyes. She didn't look at Emily as she spoke but surveyed the surroundings. They both wore the same dark green uniforms but where his hung free in the wind, hers clung to her curvaceous body. "We wanted to ask you a few questions about your attack, if that's okay?"

"Has the animal been found?" Emily smiled anxiously. She felt hope, they'd found the animal that attacked her.

"No, Miss."

Emily bit on her lip and looked away trying not to show her disappointment.

"We were wondering if you could remember anything about the animal that attacked you," the older male officer said, still chewing angrily at his gum. Emily had to look away and wondered how he could chew so loud. It reminded her of thunder off in the distance.

"Even the smallest detail could really help," Officer Myra added, stepping closer. Her shadow loomed over Emily.

"You..." Emily stammered then took a deep breath, with some success in trying to compose herself, "you still don't know what it is, do you?" They shook their heads no in unison. "I never got a look at it," she continued. "It was dark and stayed behind me. Have there been any other sightings?"

She sensed a hesitation from both officers. Then Williams spoke up, "We found a hunter. Dead. Possibly two days."

"It was days after your attack," Myra added. "Almost fifty miles northeast of the others."

"More than one?" Emily hesitated.

"Maybe. Strange for such a large animal to travel so far without being spotted at least once in daylight. It may be nocturnal," Williams' said with regret. He obviously wished he had better news.

"Everyone…who has come across this thing…has died, haven't they?"

"You were very lucky Miss Meyer," Myra said. "If anything else comes to mind, please call us." She handed over two cards, their names neatly stamped above their contact numbers.

Emily watched as they walked to their jeep. She did a quick calculation. Fifty miles northeast of where she was attacked? If it was the same animal, it was even closer. She began to panic thinking about it. Emily grabbed her book and went back inside, settling on the living room couch.

"How are you feeling?"

Ashley's voice startled her. "You scared the shit out of me!" Emily placed a hand on her chest, her heart raced.

"Sorry." Ashley sipped her coffee

"Been up long?"

"Long enough." She lifted the cup with both hands taking another drink. "I'm sure they'll find the animal and put it down."

"I hope you're right." Emily set her book on the nearby table, her heart still racing. "I'm going to take a shower."

———◆———

EMILY SLOWLY LET her hand travel around the wound on her side. The bruising seemed more extensive, traveling down and going out of sight at her jeans. It looked much worse to her now and hurt worse too. The medication was doing little to take away the pain. Her entire body ached from within. Touching the tender flesh around the wound sent pulsing shocks up her entire body causing her to bite hard on her lip.

"You're going to drive yourself crazy if you keep worrying it. Besides, dudes dig scars." Ashley stood in the doorway dressed as she was the day before.

"No," Emily mocked picking the black t-shirt from the counter and pulling it on. "Chick's dig scars. Guys prefer flawless."

"You need to date better guys," Ashley countered with a smile.

"Are you leaving?" Emily noted the keys in her hand.

"Be back before sunset. I'm not letting you spend the night alone."

"I'll be okay if you want to sleep in your own bed tonight." Emily felt embarrassed. She suddenly wanted to spend time alone.

"I know. But you could use a couple nights with someone looking out for you." Ashley gave her a quick hug and then left.

Emily waited until Ashley was gone before pulling her shirt up again, using the mirror to see from the back. She placed her hand over the wound careful not to touch it again. The bite was more than double the size of her hand.

The doorbell echoed through the home. Emily quickly crossed through the bedroom, into the living room approaching the front door. She opened it expecting Ashley.

Her hand twitched when she saw him—all six feet of him with short sandy brown hair spiked only in the front. He leaned against the doorframe with an eager smile, his shallow green eyes accentuated by his moisturized clean-shaven face. The gold chain around his neck sparkled in the light almost distracting her from the hideous green-and-black-striped polo—a size too small even on his wiry frame—with half the collar standing straight up. The tip of a frat-boy tattoo peeked through the open neck of the shirt. He looked at her with cocky swagger.

"Hello sweetheart." His big-toothed grin and strong cologne smacked her in the face as the fall air swirled through the open door.

"What do you want, Troy?" She turned leaving the door open behind her.

"I came to see you. Heard about the accident." He took a couple steps into the room.

"Ashley would kick your ass if she knew." She turned to glare at him.

"That's why I waited for her to leave. Didn't want to cause a scene." He stood in the middle of the room with that big knowing grin, his most attractive attribute and he knew it.

"Hell, she'll kick *my* ass for letting you in."

"Don't tell her." Troy crossed his arms across his chest and took a couple more steps. "The place looks the same. Except you took our picture down."

Emily glanced guiltily toward the empty space on the wall. "Didn't want to be reminded all the time," Emily hissed. She circled the counter, putting it between them.

Troy slid onto one of the stools. He placed a bottle on the counter and pushed it toward her.

"Cherry brandy," he offered. "Your favorite." He leaned over the counter, making no effort to hide his appreciative eyes roving over her figure.

Emily picked up the bottle—surprised he'd actually brought an unopened expensive version of the liquor—then she set it back down. "Used to be my favorite." She slid it back to him. "But I lost my taste for it."

"Liar." Troy laughed. "You might've lost your taste for the Troy, but not cherry brandy."

She rolled her eyes at his reference to himself.

"The addiction's still there," he murmured, like a dare. "Your mouth's watering even now, just looking at it."

Emily frowned, knowing he was right.

"One shot for old time's sake," he tempted. He was out of his seat and in the kitchen before she could refuse. He pulled out two medium glasses from the top shelf.

Emily backed away but found herself in the corner of the cabinets. He went to the freezer, trapping her in the corner, and put three cubes of ice in each glass. He hummed as he filled both glasses. The smell of the liquor caused her to wet her lips.

She knew what he was doing. He was trying to get a smile out of her and unfortunately, it was working.

"To past loves and future adventures." He handed her one glass.

She took it, careful not to touch his hand and watched him take a sip before following suit. The liquor had a bite all its own, strong with a lingering aftertaste but smooth going down. She pushed the glass back at him, feeling woozy.

Troy smiled as he placed her glass on the counter. "Don't remember you being such a light weight."

"You don't know me anymore. Never did, really," Emily shot back, fire in her eyes.

"I tried calling you," Troy countered. "Wanted to make things right." He took a large sip from his glass before he set it back down.

She took her glass from the counter, sipping more of the heady liquid before placing it beside his. She couldn't deny her anticipation as he refilled them both. She smiled. In the two years they'd gone out, the one thing he was always good at was keeping her glass full. He had a charm she couldn't resist mostly to do with his sly cocky smile.

"Can you blame me? Really?" Emily swirled the brandy around in the glass, noticing how he'd moved a step closer when she wasn't watching.

"I tried to apologize that week but your little guard dog kneed me in the balls the day I showed."

"You cheated on me! She was being a loyal friend." Her face flushed from the alcohol and anger building inside her.

"I was a bastard," he admitted, sheepishly. "But I've changed." Troy took another step forward. Emily glanced down at the tan colored tile floor seeing how much space he had closed between them. She fidgeted in her stance; he had her hemmed into the corner of the cabinets. There was no escape.

Emily angrily swallowed half the glass at once this time. "So, what? You think you can come over, catch me happy to be fucking alive, get me liquored up, and get in my pants?"

"I was worried about you."

"I can always tell when you were lying." She smirked. She ran her thumb across his eyebrow. "Your eye twitches when you lie. You were never good at hiding it once I began to notice."

"No, really. I was worried, beautiful." Troy leaned closer, their bodies almost touching now. "I came to see you there. In the hospital. But it would have been a bad idea."

Emily felt the heat radiating off him, making her uncomfortable and excited at the same time.

"Everyone there hated me, all your family, and friends. I got as far as the hospital parking lot before I talked myself out of going in." He downed the last drop of his drink and quickly refilled both their glasses again.

Emily couldn't resist any longer and reached forward to fix his collar. "Tell me, could you look like a bigger dick?" She gestured to his shirt and the gold chain necklace, and he began to laugh. She gave him a mocking smirk and lifted her glass to take another drink.

"Really, I'm sorry," Troy said in earnest. "You know I actually cried when I heard what happened. You can't imagine how happy I was when I heard you woke up."

Emily found herself lost in his eyes. She'd always loved his eyes, their light green irises. The way his lips parted as he smiled. It was all a physical attraction with Troy. It was hard for her to explain to others. He was good in bed. She had often described him in her own mind as a selfish pretty boy. He moisturized his skin—how many guys did that? —she always won but the way he kissed. He always knew what it was he wanted. And wasn't afraid to go for it. She could feel her own temperature rise as memories of the two of them flooded her mind. The wound he'd inflicted on her the year before now seemed unimportant.

"It makes you think, you know. About a lot of things…the way we ended, what a dick I was," Troy's leg bumped her knee and she tried to shift away, but there was nowhere to go.

"You sound like you're' the one who nearly died." Emily finished off her brandy rattling the ice around the empty glass. She reached for the bottle pouring it half way up and quickly downed another drink. Feeling the heat from his body, barely enough room for her to move one way or another. She bit her lip. She shouldn't have let him in. He was too dangerous…the look in his eyes, the heat between the two of them, and that knowing grin on his face. Against her better judgment, she moved in slowly and kissed him on the lips. Just a taste. But it was enough.

Troy pushed closer, reaching his hands down onto her hips and lifting her to the counter. Her gaze locked onto his. Her breath came quicker. Giving in, Emily draped her arms over his shoulders leaning in. His face hovered closer to her neck and she whimpered at the feel of his lips on her skin just below her ear. His hands were warm where they rested on her legs. Emily stared at the wall without seeing it, following the sensation of his lips on her bare skin.

"You're right," she whispered. "Being that close to death. It does make you think." She pushed him back. "Like about how this is a mistake." She stared intently at him, confused by her own thoughts. She wanted him though she knew it was wrong.

Undeterred, he pulled his shirt off and tossed it to the floor. Several new tattoos adorned his muscular chest. The star tattooed on his upper chest was a fraternity mark—she remembered that one. There was now also a dagger on his upper left arm, his initials—'T.A.'—for Troy Anders, on his right chest, and the word 'stud' on his lower stomach. That made Emily laugh. "You are so fucking full of yourself."

"Not all mistakes are bad ones," he murmured trying to sound sexy.

"That one is." She pointed toward the 'stud' tattoo.

"I was drunk." He smiled leaning in to kiss her. She couldn't help but kiss him back—more passionately than before—but she pulled away again, sighed and looked toward the ceiling. As she shifted on the hard countertop, he offered her another full glass of brandy. Gratefully, she took the glass and shot it back returning to him.

"I am not supposed to be drinking," she slurred. Her clothes were uncomfortable. Her temperature was high. She knew she was close to losing control.

"The Em I remember wasn't fond of doing the right thing." He drank again and turned back to her waiting lips. She gave into the lust, pulling his body closer, wrapping her legs around his hips. His lips deserted hers to glide down her throat and Emily let her head fall back against the cabinet.

"Ashley's going to kill me."

"Don't think about her." He captured her lips again, his tongue invading farther beyond propriety's boundaries as his warm hands slid up to her hips.

It felt so good to be touched. She didn't want to fight it. She kissed him back with abandon, pulling him closer. It wasn't until his hand moved under her shirt and touched her side that she snapped back to reality as pain shot through her.

Emily tried to push him back, but he was lost in desire. She shoved harder feeling trapped. When he didn't budge, she lost it thinking about the monster. How helpless she was against its attack. She would not let it happen now. She raked his face with her nails.

"Damn it, Em!"

Heedless of his yell, her mind was focused only on her wound, still throbbing from his touch.

"You cut me, you bitch," he accused.

When she finally looked at him, he held a hand to his wounded cheek. Through her own tears, she saw blood seep between his fingers. "Leave," she said, panting.

"What?"

"I said go!"

"Gladly," he growled and grabbed his shirt making no attempt to put it on, but instead placing it against his face.

Emily followed him to the door, shaking uncontrollably. She almost shut it before he could get clear and quickly locked it, placing her back to it as she held a hand on her side.

"Bastard."

<hr>

EMILY LAY ON the couch with the blanket pulled tight around her. Since Troy had left, she'd done nothing except stare out the window, though she could see little between the thick maroon curtains. An hour before dark she began to worry if Ashley would make it back.

She'd always acted as if she didn't need anyone, but right now, all she wanted was for Ashley to walk through the door. She imagined the other woman's voice in every sound that came from outside. The dream from the night before kept flashing in her mind every time she shut her eyes. The pain triggered by Troy's touch kept worsening but worse was the feeling in her chest. She wondered if this was what a panic attack felt like.

The buzz of her cell phone on the kitchen counter broke through her worry. She tossed the covers aside and leaped up. It had to be Ashley calling.

She'd only taken a couple of steps from the couch before she doubled over in pain, an intense hunger deep in her stomach. She collapsed to her hands and knees. It wasn't her side that hurt so much, but hunger. An intense feeling, she realized she'd been feeling all day. She stifled a scream as she fell to her side, hands tightly across her abdomen. The pain went deeper than just hunger. Her insides seemed to shift—readjusting within her—bringing an unsettling fear.

Her heart beat three times faster and then her muscles began to spasm forcing her from her side to her back. Her hips lifted from the floor and what felt like sharp pieces of glass cut through every muscle along her torso. She dropped her hips back to the floor rolling over onto her stomach. Every part of her screamed in agony all the way to her throat and jaws. She wheezed two breaths before she began to choke. Her fingernails dug into the hardwood, breaking as she tried to pull herself forward. Her jaw muscles throbbed, each tooth felt like needles were being stuck through her gums. She rose from the floor and vomited a mix of brandy and food. Coughing through her tight chest, she threw up again. This time only a white foamy substance escaped as her arms buckled beneath her. She curled up in a ball and drifted out of consciousness.

6

EACH BREATH WAS *a mix of harsh cold air and wetness, the taste of a fresh rain on her tongue. It was nearly pitch black, a thick fog, but she still had no problem seeing the path. The ground below was rough but did not hinder her progress, with every dozen steps there was a pause. A glance to the sky, the harsh red haze of the sun as it would break the mountaintops in the next hour. The very thought caused her heart to race, as again she took to the trail. She was nearly out of time. The rain bounced off her, kept her cool from the run. The fresh air engulfed all her senses; the forest was alive with animals and foliage. Neither of those were the scent she hunted. It was there, the familiar smell of a person. She leaped through the wilderness at an exceptional speed, did not slow to even look to the path. The scent was so close, soared again through more brush and under several crossed logs before she slid to a stop turning to the very spot she had just crossed. She could smell his blood now. Feel the familiar heat of his body. She heard him whimper when their eyes met and she leaped.*

Emily opened her eyes. The familiar ceiling greeted her. Taking a deep breath, she barely moved. She could hear one voice echoing in her mind. She flashbacked to being a kid—when she would pretend to be asleep during one of her parent's late-night arguments—which were almost always about her. She wasn't a straight A student. Track was the only thing she ever truly excelled at. Nevertheless, a B average on top of the demands of track and field hadn't been enough for her father. Over his voice she heard the beep of the heart monitor and felt the pinch on her left arm where the IV taped to her skin pierced her vein.

Emily shifted. She tried desperately to hear what they were saying without letting them know she was awake.

"She's awake."

It only took a moment before her parents towered over her. Her dad was on the right side of the bed and her mom on the left. She felt like she was twelve again and just got caught kissing Tommy Jacobs behind the church. She lifted her head up seeing Ashley across the room secluded in a chair. The expression on her friend's face spoke volumes—a face filled with worry and anger. Mostly Emily could see the guilt written all over her face. Emily's heart sank. Her best friend was blaming herself.

"You are going to have to stop scaring us." Her mom placed a tight grip on her hand. Her eyes were bloodshot.

"What happened?" Emily questioned. Her throat was sore and ached with both words.

"We're hoping you could tell us," Ashley replied.

Emily looked to her again, still across the room in the chair. She was so close but felt like Ashley was a mile away.

"I came back and found you on the floor *alone.*"

She was indeed alone but the bite Ashley put on the last word let Emily know what she'd already figured out. Ashley knew about Troy. She could handle her parents being disappointed and mad at her, but not Ash.

"How long have I been here?"

"Three days. The doctor ran a series of tests on your blood, cat scans, everything…but he couldn't tell us why you were unconscious. Everything came back normal," her dad stated, taking a seat beside her. His grip on her hand was tighter than her mother's. "You were transferred back to Charleston when you were stable, to the same hospital and doctors as before."

"They are going to keep you in here for a few days, sweetie, and see if they can figure out why you had a seizure," her mom stated.

It came back to her now—the pain she was in, how every muscle in her body seemed to rip apart. The dream she had while asleep came back to her too. The person she had attacked was Troy. What was that dream about…she knew she was angry at Troy before the seizure.

"I'm sorry."

"It's not your fault, sweetie." Her mom used her free hand to wipe away strands of her messed up red hair.

"The doctor said it could have been a reaction to the medicine you're on and stress." Her dad glanced toward Ashley. "Or something you ate or drank, or a mix of all the above."

She gave her friend a sad smile as their eyes met. She knew she had missed a confrontation between Ashley and her father.

"I'll go tell the doctor you're awake." Ashley quickly left the room.

"You need to try to go back to sleep," her mom said, her hand still on her daughter's forehead.

"Don't blame Ashley…" Emily said, staring at the ceiling for only a moment before looking at her father. Emily could hear him grit his teeth. She could imagine the scolding he had given Ashley must have been especially degrading. But, she imagined the one he wanted to give her this second was much worse.

"We'll talk about that later."

His jaw unclenched, but she thought she could almost hear his heart race with anger as he let her hand go, leaving the room. Emily would not tell them about the visit from Troy, especially since it seemed Ashley had not either. Her parents and best friend had not always gotten along. They considered her a bad influence on their daughter despite the fact that in their youth Emily was the more outgoing and wilder of the two. One thing the three of them always agreed on was their dislike of Troy. At times, even she had a hard time remembering what she saw in him.

"Get some sleep." Her mom placed a hand on her cheek. "I'm going to check on your father."

Emily waited until she was gone before placing her hand on the wound on her left side. She flinched at the touch of her cold fingers, but it was due to habit more than pain. For the first time she could remember, the pain was gone. She ran her hand up and down her side without so much as a sting. She could not fight back the large smile as Ashley walked back into the room.

"You owe me," she muttered crossing the room and taking a seat beside the bed.

"I don't feel it anymore," she stated.

"What do you mean?" Ashley questioned.

"The bite on my side… It doesn't hurt like it did." Emily smiled looking to her friend. She slowly reached her free hand out, placing it on Ashley's knee.

"You had me worried," Ashley replied. "When I came home…. you were still shaking on the floor. You were hot to the touch—like blistering hot." Her voice dropped low, "And you were foaming at the fucking mouth…"

Emily lost her smile as she heard the last part.

"I am worried about you. I told the doctor about all of this. I had to. That is one of the reasons he ran so many tests on you—after they got your fever to break. They thought you may have rabies or something, but everything came back clear." Ashley turned looking toward the door before she spoke next, "And why the fuck did you let him in the house?" She looked back at her friend with a disapproving glare.

"I thought it was you…" she paused. "He was at the door almost the moment you left; so, I never even thought to check who was on the other side, I just opened…. then it was too late."

"I'm guessing the two of you almost drank half a bottle of brandy too," Ashley specified.

"Don't be mad," Emily said.

"Kind of hard not to be." Ashley nervously looked back at the door. "You let that ass back into your life after what you just went through. He is no good for you."

"Nothing happened we just had a few drinks," Emily quickly replied. She would not tell her friend the whole story. "And I don't expect to see him anytime soon."

"Good," Ashley replied leaning back in her chair. "You are really starting to scare me."

"I've never felt anything like that," Emily stated. It never occurred to her until now; she had been feeling different, ill the entire day up until the seizure. "I had no control over what my body was doing...and then there are the dreams. They have been so real."

"You're going to be in here for a few days and I hate to say this but maybe talking to the psychiatrist isn't a bad idea."

Emily smiled at her friend's words. It was an uneasy smile. She knew her best friend and father were right. She, at least, took relief if Ashley thought so.

<hr>

EMILY WOKE. IT was dark with only the light from the television and the monitors to illuminate the room. The curtains were pulled closed but it was not hard to tell it was also pitch dark outside. It was then she saw the figure sitting in the dark across the room.

"I hope I didn't startle you," the voice proclaimed.

She watched as the shadowy figure reached and turned the light on and she immediately knew it was Dr. Knox.

"What are you doing sitting here in the dark?" Emily questioned sitting up in the bed to get a better look at the other woman.

"I wanted to monitor you sleeping," Knox stated, as she leaned back in her chair.

"Where are the others?" Emily quickly asked.

"Your parents went home after some convincing from your friend, as for the spitfire, she's here somewhere," Knox said with a smile.

There was a story there. Emily would surely hear about later from Ashley.

"I heard you have been having nightmares."

"Violent ones," Emily replied breaking eye contact. There was a familiarity here—though before the other day she had never met Dr. Knox in person—she had overheard a lot about her during parents more troubled years of marriage.

"Not uncommon," Knox stated, "after what you've been through."

"I know I'm lucky," Emily replied.

"Yes, you are a lucky young woman, but I don't think you truly know how lucky you are," Knox said. She turned and picked up a paper. It wasn't the front page of the local paper but the back section. She approached the bed and handed the paper over.

Her picture was on the front page of the November 1st paper, as the only survivor in a string of animal attacks. The back page talked about the victim total, which was now up to seven in less than a month.

"They still don't know what it is," Knox stated, "and the attacks are only getting more frequent." She pulled the chair at the side of the bed closer and took a seat. The older woman was dressed very much the same as the first time they met except the dress jacket was across the room on the other chair. She wore a silk white dress shirt and plain black business skirt. "More than ever it'll be present in your thoughts and if you need anyone to talk to about it, or anything, you can talk to me."

"I had a dream the animal was in my home the other night. It was so real—right down to Ashley's blood. It was like nothing I have ever felt from a dream…" Emily paused looking at her own clasped hands, "And then I had another after my seizure."

"What was it about?" Knox questioned.

Emily shook thinking about both dreams but she almost lost her breath thinking of the second. "I was the animal." Emily slowly glanced to the doctor before again glaring at the muted television. "Is that strange?"

"In this dream, you were the one with the power correct?" Knox questioned. Emily noticed how uneasy Knox seemed. She wondered what she was thinking. Likely that she was crazy, which gave Emily an uneasy feeling of her own.

"I killed someone in the dream." Emily's lip quivered. Knox still seemed calm even with what she just heard.

"Who?" Knox questioned.

"Is that really something you need to know?" Emily inquired.

"Anything you tell me stays between us," Knox quickly replied.

"So, am I your patient now?" Emily questioned in a vague attempt at changing the subject.

"Simply put, yes, you are," Knox answered.

"Is Dad paying you?" Emily questioned looking away from the other woman.

"Yes, but that is between him and me and I will not tell him anything you say to me either. Anything you tell me is between us," Knox stated. "Now tell me, who was it you killed?"

"My ex-boyfriend," Emily replied.

"And why was he the victim, something in your subconscious?" Knox questioned.

"The night of my seizure…he was at my home. You and Ashley are the only people who know this," Emily replied, leaning back in her bed, and staring up at the ceiling.

"And the two of you fought." Knox observed.

"It was more than that. Things did not end well between us before. And the other night we had a little bit to drink. I had just survived the attack. We started making out…and when he touched my side, I lost it. Scratched his face…"

"So you're angrier at yourself than him," Knox replied.

"I'm mad at him, but yes…I should have never let him back in my life. The moment I knew it was him, I should have slammed the door in his face. But, I didn't…I let him in and almost made a huge mistake. No matter how disappointed Ashley may be in me, it does not compare to how I feel." Emily could not fight back the tears.

"Ashley seems like a good friend. Maybe it's possible she is mad at herself for not being there to make sure he was not allowed in more than she is disappointed in you," Knox said matter-of-factly.

Emily paused. "Maybe."

"The dreams are normal—call it survivor's guilt—and until you find peace with what happened, they may continue. They may even get worse before they get better," Knox stated. "The first thing you need to remember is they are just dreams and they can't hurt you."

"Doesn't change how real they feel," Emily replied.

"Between reality and nightmares there's often a thin line of subconsciousness. I would be more worried if you begin to daydream in the same manner," Knox stated. "I could prescribe you some sleeping pills—may help you get a deeper sleep—but I can't promise the dreams won't be worse."

"Could that mean longer more fucked up dreams?" Emily questioned with a pause, "Sorry for my language."

"No worries, and yes, there is a possibility a deeper sleep could lead to longer and more terrifying dreams," Knox replied.

"I think I'll take my chances without the pills," Emily countered.

"Anything else you want to talk about?" Knox questioned.

Emily only nodded, "No."

EMILY WOKE, THE air suffocating as if smoke had filled her lungs. The door was open wide. She could hear the flicker of industry lights. Shadows danced around the room violently as she sat up in her bed. A chill overtook her body. She was alone in the room. She sat back for only a moment. The silence was deafening. It was then she looked at the monitor by her bedside—even it was dark and silent. A quick glimpse at her arm and only the bandage remained where the IV once pierced skin leaving the red irritation from the needle. "Hello," she called out pushing the assistance button on her bed. She waited… and waited, but no one came. She twisted her legs from under the thin sheets and to the cold floor. She glanced around the room for something—anything—to wear other than the hospital gown.

Emily turned the light on and instantly the room lit up and out as the bulbs blew. "Damn it," she mumbled. She gave two quick clicks of the switch with no reaction. By the door was a small duffel bag. She peeked inside and smiled when she saw the contents—flannel pajama pants. With no hesitation, she pulled them free and up her slender legs. Only a moment later she tied the strings tight so they hugged against her skin. With one last scan of the duffel bag, she pulled out a shredded t-shirt—it was ripped as if someone had taken scissors to it—and she realized these were not her clothes. "Ashley," she called out with shirt in hand, rushing to the bathroom, turning the light on and looking around for her friend. A big sigh of relief escaped when she saw nothing in the room. "Wake up," she whispered, "wake up damn it, I cannot do this again."

Emily quickly pulled the gown free when nothing changed. The cold air on her bare skin caused an instant shiver and chill bumps covered her upper body. She pulled Ashley's shirt over her head. The rips in the shirt left her breasts partially exposed, as well as her midriff. Every cut in the shirt allowed icy air to assault her bare skin. "Come on Ash, were you planning on flashing half the nursing staff?" She walked across the room and to the door before she finished her thought, even though she knew her friend likely intended to wear it over another shirt. "Course you were."

Emily turned away glancing down both halls. She saw nothing "Hello, anybody there?" she called out. The floor was as cold as the air around her. She crossed her arms against her chest trying to warm them and feel less exposed to any prying eyes. "Hello," she called out again taking several steps down the hall leading toward the nurse's station. She approached, hearing the ringing of a phone but there was no one there to answer. She stepped behind the counter and picked up the phone. "Hello…" She pulled the phone away hearing the sound of loud deep breaths echoed from the other end. She placed it back to her ear. The breathing was gone but just as suddenly she heard a voice hiss, "Emily."

Without hesitation, she slammed the phone back to the counter. Instantly it rang again. The sound startled her forcing her to take several quick steps back away from the counter. She started to shiver uncontrollably as she looked around the lounge nervously. The voice on the other end of the phone was a woman's voice, raspy and hollow.

The hospital intercom came on and static filled the speakers. There was a long moment of unsettling silence in which nothing but static filled the room.

"Wake up." Emily pinched her arm, backing up to the wall. She dug her nails into her skin until it began to bleed. "Fuck."

The intercom stopped broadcasting. She crept along the wall until she was back in the open halls of the hospital and she could see the door to her room. She took a deep breath just as she broke into a run. Her bare feet slapped the hard floor echoing in the hall around her. She stopped with her hand on the handle with a crash. She twisted and turned the doorknob, pushing against the frame, but the door would not budge. "Come on," she cried out in frustration as she kicked the door.

A loud scream broke Emily from her fight with the door forcing her to turn her back against the solid surface. Her other hand now fought with the handle but still no movement. Another blood-chilling scream echoed through the hallway. This one sounded different and seemed to come from another direction.

Emily crept out into the hall away from the door. Sweat trickled down her neck and dampened her uncombed hair. "Anyone here," she called out in almost a whimper.

She heard more screams and moans, but it was different from before. Sounds of pleasure filled the hospital. "Hello." She took a few steps down the hall in the opposite direction of the nurse's station. With almost every step she looked back behind her and then toward the sound of pleasure. She approached the door. Light escaped from underneath as she twisted the handle but kept the door flush against the frame. She allowed it to crack as the moans grew louder and unhindered. She opened it farther and farther until she could see inside. A big window spied into another room—an observation room. She shut the door behind her and took a deep breath before she again started to move. A few steps into the room as silent as she could spying through the observation room glass to see the source of the erotic moans.

"Ashley," she whispered. Emily watched as her friend sat upon someone else. Ashley's back bare except for a tattoo of a crow perched on a cross was to the mirror. It was her only tattoo, but it spanned from shoulder to shoulder, covering most of her upper back. She'd always planned on getting others, but only if they had meaning…like the crow. A representation of her Cherokee Grandfather.

Emily could clearly see the other woman now, Vanessa Myra, the Wildlife Enforcement officer. Vanessa's eyes closed in the moment of passion. Emily could only smile watching the two in their most sensual moments. Vanessa pushed Ashley backward until she was flat on her back. Ashley's back arched from the bed as the other woman disappeared under the covers. Her petite frame lifted farther from the bed as her jaw opened. She ran her hands across her small breasts and dark nipples, up her collarbone and finally stopped at her throat. Emily watched as her tiny fingers began to dig at her own throat and instantly she turned away. Emily began to breathe harder and wheeze with each breath. With her back to the mirror, she could hear the moans of pleasure intensify from the room.

It was a few breaths before Emily began to feel the calm within her own chest—before she felt comfortable enough to turn and look back at the room. She smiled as she saw them. Vanessa sat up and looked toward her. Ashley's legs wrapped around the woman's waist as she too looked toward Emily. The mischievous smile of her friend almost made her blush. There was very little of Ashley left to her imagination as she turned, twisting her body to look back at Emily.

Emily gasped. Behind them, the shadows came alive as a dark figure stalked the lovers. "Behind You!" Emily yelled. She grabbed a chair and turning to put her weight into the movement, she threw it at the observation window. It bounced back to the floor at her feet with a loud crash, but the glass was unharmed. Where once lovers lay now only sheets remained.

"Fuck!" Emily screamed. "Ashley," she mumbled again scratching at her own arm.

Emily, backing to the door, kept an eye on the room. She looked down the hallway she had traveled before; the light still flickered outside of her room. She glanced at her left arm. A wound, caused by her own hand, dripped blood onto the floor below. "Please just wake up," she said out loud. She began to look around for a weapon—any kind of weapon. She stepped back into the observation room and looked through every drawer but found nothing she could use. It was then she saw the fire extinguisher. She rushed to pick it up and remove the safety key. She held the hose high as she clicked the trigger spraying it over the mirror. She could still remember what she had watched in the room moments before.

"Dreams can't hurt you," she mumbled rushing out of the room and into the hall. Her heart pounded in her throat as she yelled, "Come and get me. I'm not afraid of you anymore." It was a lie; she was terrified. Even though she was wholly convinced, this was a dream she was still frightened.

She walked toward the nurse's station. It was then she saw the bloodied footprints on the floor as they came from her own room and headed toward the station. They were not the tracks of an animal but those of small feet. She followed them as they crossed in front of the counter and to an elevator. She stepped inside the opened door and could see a bloody print on the button for the first floor. Emily pressed the button and the doors closed. The elevator began its descent as static from the radio bounced around the small space. She set the extinguisher on the floor and pulled her hair back into a ponytail. The door opened. Emily grabbed the fire extinguisher and stepped out into the main room of the hospital. It was the emergency room and it looked like a trash dump as papers floated on the wind. Chairs and tables were knocked over, trashcans were scattered about and old magazines lay everywhere on the tiled floor.

She had no problem following the tracks heading toward the back of the hospital and to a separate elevator. She knew almost on instinct where this elevator led—the mortuary. She stepped inside following the same pattern as before with the quick close and movement of the elevator. The door opened and she could hear the sounds of voices. A calming male voice whispered on the air. She knew it instantly. Colin was here…

Emily slowly walked through the doors. She saw him as he walked across the morgue without a stitch of clothing on. She'd never seen him naked before…but his manhood was on display for to see now. She stepped through the last of the doors between them. She wanted this to be different from the vision she had of Ashley. If the animal was here, she would stop it…and hopefully wake from the nightmare.

Colin turned to her and smiled. "Darling it is good for you to join us!"

Emily paused. "Us?" She looked around the room but saw no one else. She looked back at Colin, trying to focus on his shaggy blond hair and a half beard but she couldn't stop her eyes from drifting down his thin frame. His toned body for her to see as she never had before.

"Like what you see, Red?" he questioned, spreading his arms wide for a hug.

He had taken several steps forward before she saw the woman sitting in a fetal position on the floor behind Colin. Emily glared over her crossed arms at her. She did not know this person—or at least, in her current position, she could not make out who she was.

"I always thought you would make a great lay, or so my brother told me as much," he said.

Emily opened her mouth wanting to speak but nothing came out. She hadn't thought about Colin's older brother in a long time. She looked back at the woman and then Colin. He was several steps away but he continued his approach until he was pressed against her. He wrapped his arms around her and kept walking until her back was against the door.

"Colin, we have to go," Emily muttered, looking into his eyes. She could feel his ice-cold hands against her bare stomach as his fingers ran across the bandage on her left side.

"No fun."

He lowered kissing her on the lips. Her eyes were wide open as she allowed the kiss to happen.

"We have time for a quickie, darling."

"I'm dreaming, Colin…this is not real," she muttered.

"Feels all real to me." He placed his hands on her breasts and rubbed her hard nipples between his fingers. "And all too nice."

"Fuck," she mumbled.

"That is the idea," he replied kissing her again.

Their tongues caressed one another but she continued to keep her eyes open and watched the woman on the opposite side of the room. More importantly, she watched for the animal. It was here. It had to be here…why else was she here?

The fire extinguisher clanked loudly as it hit the floor, but Emily never even realized she dropped it. Emily felt Colin's hands run down the back of her flannel pajamas to firmly grip her ass and lift her to his own hips. Tight against his erection she could feel it between them rubbing against her inner thigh.

"Snap out of it, Emily," she said out loud. She clung to him, one arm draped over his shoulders as he nibbled and licked her neck. "Colin," she whispered into his ear. It was becoming harder for her to fight the feeling in her stomach. Terror was being replaced with lust. "Colin," she said again. She had never thought of her friend in this manner before—they had always been just friends. It was his brother she had a relationship with; that was how they met.

"Love it when you say my name," he stated, kissing her just below her ear.

"We cannot stay here," she muttered. With her back pressed to the wall, there was no room to breathe between their bodies.

"We are safe here. Only the dead will see us here," Colin stated with a laugh running his tongue up her neck slowly to savor the taste of her sweat and excitement.

"And her…" Emily paused. She could still see the other woman across the room. She had not moved, and their eyes were now glued on one another. Distinct green eyes stared back at her.

Colin turned to look at her. "I never even realized she was here."

Colin paused as he released his grip and Emily's bare feet touched the ice-cold tile floor sending a chill up her entire body. She knew this was a dream, she fought to try to wake, but it seemed pointless.

She walked past Colin though she could feel him linger only steps behind as she approached the other woman. "Hello…" Emily said stopping at the table where on any given day a medical examiner would autopsy a body. "Do I know you?" she questioned. She knew she had to; it was the only way she could be in this dream.

Emily felt Colin's hands on her bare stomach and felt him rub against her backside. His hand traveled back around to her hips, pulling her a couple of steps back. Shifting her step to the left, he pushed her hard against the table.

"Damn it, Colin," she shifted her body to try to see what he was doing as he kissed her on her lower back and again used his tongue to run slowly up her body. "This is not the time for this." She turned forward for a moment and looked to the woman who seemed to have no reaction to what was happening in front of her. Of course she didn't… it was a dream. It was the same reason Colin was being so aggressive when he had not a single aggressive bone in his body.

Emily felt the tug at her pajama's but the string held tight and she heard him mumble as he tugged again. She felt his hand against the inside of her legs. "Ok this has got to stop." She could not fight back the grin or the laughter as she pushed his hand away. She stood straight and turned to face him. "Any other time I would fully welcome a good dream fuck, but this—this is not you—and I don't know her. Only a moment ago, I watched Ashley with a woman upstairs and then"—she had momentarily lost focus on why she came down to the morgue— "the bloody tracks." She smacked at Colin's hand reaching out to grab at the string on her pants. "Down boy." Her eyes wandered down his chest and flat stomach.

It came from nowhere, and blood sprayed across the room and over Emily's face. Colin fell to the floor, his left leg dangled and most of his crotch and stomach was gone. She still did not see the animal. She stared in silence into Colin's open eyes as they looked back at hers. She could not say a word or muster a scream. Shock had taken her.

Emily heard the sound of flesh being torn; slowly she turned her head and could see the bloody mess against the wall from where the woman's throat had been ripped open. Still no animal in sight. The beep of the elevator opening broke her from the shock. She no longer looked at Colin. Running to the door and picking the fire extinguisher up she charged the elevator door. It shut just as she reached it. She watched as it lifted and repeatedly clicked on the button for it to return. She turned with her back against the wall. The tracks were there again. She knew it was an animal but the tracks coming from the room and into the elevator were human.

Emily rushed in when the door opened. She clicked the button for the ground level as she looked at the floor. It was covered in tracks—all human. As the door to the ground level opened she sprayed the extinguisher, but nothing was there. The tracks were easy to see leading back to the other elevator, a return track from the way she traveled before. Emily followed suit back to the floor where her room waited. As the door opened all of the lights around the nurse's station flickered much like the one outside her room earlier. "I know you are here," she yelled.

Emily stepped out and immediately saw the mangled body to her right. The persons face was mauled and unrecognizable, but she knew whom it was. "This is just a dream." The jacket the man wore was the same one he wore on the day of her graduation. It was her father. She turned away determined not to look back but she could not stop. One last look before she passed by the corner of the nurse's station. A swinging door ahead moved with the wind. Emily ran down the hall and through the doors—and almost fell in the puddle of blood on the other side. Another body lay against the wall. Another body lay against the wall, chest caved into a bloody mess, but fact still intact, her mother's face. She had seen the dead bodies of all those she cared about and her heart raced. She could not bring herself to even try to pinch herself awake again. Just considering it caused her to glance to the scrapes on her left arm from earlier. She ran down the hall chasing the only stable light around. She slowed reaching the large double doors of a surgical room of some sort. She slowly turned the knob and stepped inside. She held a tight ready grip to the trigger of the extinguisher. A third body lay just inside the room. Troy. He was naked and most of his lower body was bloodied and shredded. It was a dream. She was certain of that. She would not let herself mourn for the others, but seeing Troy's mangled body brought a sinister smile to her lips.

Emily could hear the sound of flesh being pulled and torn from the other side of the operating table. A step to the left revealed the blank expression of Doctor Knox, cold on the floor. It was then she saw her…the animal. Naked and lean the woman towered over the open wound in Knox's stomach. Organs were being pulled, ripped, and eaten from the older woman.

The sound of gnawing and splatter made Emily's stomach turn. "What are you?" she muttered and the sounds halted. She could see the woman had stopped eating but made no other movement. "What the fuck are you?" Emily called out louder. She watched as the woman stood—white, with pale skin, lean runner's legs, and a petite body. It was then she noticed the long, flowing, curly red hair. A glance at her own hair made her heart skip a beat. Emily watched. She was looking into her own eyes. Her hair, her lips, her face…mouth and chin covered in blood and skin. Her neck and chest were also covered in blood. It dripped from her mouth and body to the floor below. The other Emily's head tilted to one side—her eyes feral and wild like a rabid animal—a curious glare trying to figure out what it was she was seeing.

Emily took a step back, and on instinct, the other took a step forward. She took another step and felt her feet slip out from under her. Emily fell flat on her back. Before she could move, she was being straddled by the naked body of her other self. She felt the woman's nose against her neck as she pinned her arms to the floor. She could feel blood as it dripped on her face causing an intense shiver. She dared not move. Now she looked up into the woman's eyes. It was almost like looking in a mirror but there was something different in her eyes. Anger looked down at her—lips parted so she could see the large blood-stained canines—and in that instant, she felt them pierce into the soft skin of her neck.

8

EMILY SAT UP immediately. She placed a hand on her neck. She was covered in a cold sweat. She paused seeing the woman at her bedside. She paused seeing the woman at her bedside. Her short brown hair was chopped off at the neck, light pink lipstick accentuated a sly smile, and distinct green eyes stared back at Emily. It was her—the woman from the morgue.

"You seemed to be sleeping peacefully," she said, her lips parting in a smile. She wore nurse's scrubs. She closed the book she'd been reading and placed it on her lap, but not before folding the page to mark her place.

Emily tried to speak but nothing came out.

"Here." The woman handed over a cup of water. "Your friend Ashley asked me to sit with you while she ran out. She'll be back soon."

"Who are you?" Emily questioned after a drink.

"I'm Lauren." The woman leaned forward in her chair. "Um…I know Ashley. Ash has told me a lot about you."

Emily smiled when she said 'Ash'. Ashley would only allow those really close to her to call her by the short version of her name, for all others it was the full pronunciation.

"You seemed to be dreaming. What was it about?"

Emily now remembered where she had seen the nurse before. She was one of those who were there when she woke up from the coma. Emily paused. "Nothing important." She would not tell a stranger about this dream. She would not tell her parents, friends, or Knox about this particular dream. She tried to wrap her mind around the fact that she was the animal. She tried to wrap her mind around the fact that she was the animal…and the fact that now she was awake, she felt awkwardly calm. It was as if a weight had been lifted off her shoulders. The truth had been revealed to her, somehow. "How long have I been out?"

"A couple hours."

The last thing Emily remembered before the dream was her conversation with Dr. Knox, and it felt like days since.

"Doctor Henderson says you may be released tomorrow," Lauren stated.

"That will be nice," Emily said with hesitation. There was something wrong with her even if the tests told the doctors there wasn't. She lay back in her bed and stared at the ceiling. "Do you know if my friend Colin has been here?"

"Tall, skinny, with shaggy blond hair?"

"That's him." She smiled and for a moment thought about him from the dream. There was a pause of silence in the room as Emily lost herself in thought. It was obvious when she came back to reality. Jolting back up in her bed she turned to look at the nightstand.

"What is it?" Lauren questioned.

"Do you know if my phone is here?" Emily asked.

Without replying, Lauren crossed the room and picked up a blue duffel bag, much like the one from Emily's dream, that sat just inside the door. Emily watched as the nurse sifted through the bag. She turned, holding up a cell phone. Lauren handed the phone to Emily and then returned to her seat and her book.

The phone had been turned off. Emily waited for it to boot then quickly sifted through her contacts until she rested on Colin's name.

She shot him a quick text message before settling back into a comfortable position on the bed. She set the phone back on the nightstand and crossed her arms against her chest.

"So, can I ask you a…uh question," Lauren asked.

Emily looked at her in wonder. "About me…or Ashley?" Emily grinned.

"She is single isn't she," Lauren questioned.

Emily sat up in her bed. The smile on her face was almost infectious as Lauren replied with a grin of her own.

"Ashley's last serious relationship was over a year ago. She may be spunky, flirtatious, and sometimes loud but she is faithful," Emily replied.

"To both her lovers and friends." Startled by the interruption, both Lauren and Emily quickly glanced at the door where Ashley stood. "Talk about people much?" She smiled as she crossed the room. Ashley flopped down on the edge of the bed next to Emily. "Scoot," she said, motioning for Emily to move and make equal space.

"Good to know." Lauren smiled as she glanced at her watch. "I must be checking in."

They watched as the nurse left the room. Lauren took one last glance back at them—mostly Ashley—before she was out of sight.

"I see my unfortunate accident is doing wonders for your love life," Emily replied resting her head on the woman's shoulder.

The phone on the stand beeped twice and Emily quickly reached to read the text message. She smiled before she set the phone back on the nightstand.

"If that was from Troy I swear after I beat him into a coma and you are healthy enough I'll put you right back in this hospital bed."

"Text from Colin, just checking in," Emily replied allowing her head to return to its previous position. She watched as Ashley moved her legs over top of her own. "You don't have to worry about Troy. I don't plan on ever seeing him again." There was a pause between them. Emily took a long deep breath. "I hope Dad didn't say hurtful things to you?"

"He did," Ashley said. She began to play with a loose string on the ripped part of her jeans. "But I understood how it looked…the alcohol in your system…I was supposed to be keeping an eye on you. I'm not sure if he'll trust me to be the one to look after you the next few days when you get out though."

"Not his choice."

"How did the therapy session go?" Ashley questioned.

Emily half smiled, she would not press to find out exactly what her father had said. "Wasn't really a session—I mean it didn't last an hour or anything we just chatted," Emily replied.

"Are you going to see her again?"

"I don't know." Emily twisted lying back on the bed. "I think you should get some sleep." She watched as her friend kissed her on the forehead before turning off the light on the nightstand. Emily did not want to go to sleep—not after the dream—but Emily didn't want to go to sleep—not after the dream—she fell asleep the moment her eyes closed.

❖

EMILY HEARD THE chatter in the other room—her mother and Ashley—but she could not make out what was being said. Another voice cut into the conversation…a familiar feminine voice. A moment later, a knock came at the door. It opened and Ashley stepped inside. "Colin is on his way, he is going to take you home if that is alright with you."

"You and Lauren have a date?" Emily already knew who the third voice was but Ashley's smile confirmed her suspicions.

"Just lunch, few hours away and don't know when I'll get to see her again, but I'll be there before dark," Ashley replied. "I promise, Colin is staying with you until I get there."

"Have fun." Emily turned back to the mirror. She was astonished by her refreshed appearance, for the first time since the attack. Her hair fluffed and neat, thoroughly brushed, she had even taken the time to apply eye shadow and lip-gloss as she waited to be released from the hospital. The thing that caught her attention the most was her clothes—it should have freaked her out. She wore light blue pajama pants and a ripped-up old t-shirt over a tank top…very similar to the dream.

Emily slipped the tennis shoes over her bare feet just before she exited the room.

"How are you feeling honey?" she asked in a sweet voice only a mother uses—filled with love, compassion, and concern.

"I don't know," Emily replied honestly. "I feel…alive."

Her mom only laughed.

"I'm being serious. I am not freaking out about the attack. I can shut my eyes without having flashes of that night happening." She could not help but wonder how much of this was because of the dream.

"I'm glad," her mom replied.

"Why didn't Dad come to see me," she questioned, turning away from her mother to finish gathering the few things left on the nightstand.

"He had an emergency with a patient," she replied.

"You are looking up and spry."

Emily smiled. She knew the voice without turning. Colin was here.

"Amazing what a couple of near-death experiences will do for one's complexion," Emily replied looking over her shoulder.

Colin leaned against the door of the room. He wore a blue flannel shirt with the top three buttons undone--the color was eerily similar to the pants she wore—and loose-fitting dark jeans. Large hunting boots covered his feet. Colin was a hunter, though it was one of those things he never spoke about. It was one of the reasons Emily sent him the text message the day before.

"And cheerful," he stated with a large grin. His hands were on his hips with his thumbs hooked inside the pockets of his pants.

"I'm ready to go home," Emily said, pushing her phone—the last of her items—into the blue duffel bag on the bed, and sitting down. She glanced at the clock. It had been nearly an hour since the doctor said he would be by.

———————◆———————

EMILY SAT IN the passenger seat of the SUV—jet-black in color and most of the interior was the same with a soft suede texture. There was a light hum of music from a local country station. That was one of the few things she did not like about Colin—his taste in music.

She watched the passing wilderness and thought about what the doctor had told her, *'Any signs of a headache, nausea, unexplained illness, do not hesitate to call me.'* She was sure the doctor—though nearly twice her age—was flirting with her. Especially when he offered to be the one to push her from the hospital in the wheelchair—something Colin was quick to take responsibility for. They were just friends but Colin made it no secret he hated it when older men flirted with her, as he had witnessed quite frequently when they were out together. She always wondered if it bothered him because they flirted with her or because they did it so unapologetically with him right there...like there was no chance the two of them were an item.

"Earth to Emily."

His words broke her from her daze. She had not realized he had been talking to her the whole time.

"Did you hear anything I said?"

"I'm sorry..." she paused with a small laugh. She glanced forward realizing where they were—two miles from the spot where she lost control of her car. Ashley had purposely avoided taking her this direction the last time she was released. "Could you stop up ahead?"

"You sure that is a good idea," Colin questioned.

"Please." She placed a hand on his as it sat in the space between them. She knew how to play Colin. And 'please' always worked wonders.

"No one can know we came this way. Your mother asked me to go the long way. I don't know why I let you talk me into this," Colin said.

They traveled the remaining distance. There was nowhere close for them to get off the road at the site of the accident, but Colin pulled over a few hundred feet away. Emily was out of the vehicle, walking up the side of the road, almost before he put it in park. He ran up behind her.

"This isn't a good idea."

"You can stay in the truck if you want." She laughed, picking up the pace of her walk. They walked the curve and could see where it happened and almost instantly, she paused.

"Are you ok?" Colin questioned placing a hand on her shoulder.

"I'll be fine," she replied again starting to walk. She did not stop again until she was at the scene of the accident and a few steps down the hill where she was attacked. "The guy who saved me…did you ever hear his name?"

"Mathew Bradley."

Emily turned to look at Colin.

"You happened to remember it so bluntly?" she questioned.

"I know the guy," Colin replied.

Emily was shocked.

"I've met him in passing; he was hunting buddies with my dad a long time ago. I haven't seen him in years and until the day of your accident, I hadn't even heard his name in years.

"You sure it's the same guy then?" Emily questioned turning away and a few more steps down the embankment. She was amazed with how much time had passed that she could still see the skid marks and deep treads where she spun.

"I'm sure. They described him to me. I wanted to be sure it was him," Colin replied. "How much do you know about what happened?"

"Very little. I do know he never saw the animal," Emily replied.

"Lauren—the cute nurse Ashley is taking out—told me he carried you into the emergency room that night, covered in your blood. Lauren was just coming on duty. She said the man was pale as a ghost like he had seen something but he could hardly speak," Colin stated.

"You think he saw something?" she questioned.

"I think he was in shock from finding a young woman half dead in the middle of the road," Colin stated standing by her side.

"Could you take me to him?" she questioned.

"I know where he lives but I doubt he will be there...but this time of the year I think I know where we could find him," Colin stated. "But not today."

"Tomorrow then?" she questioned. She turned walking past him. She paused at the roadside and waited for a car to pass. When the crossing was clear, she spoke again, "I have another favor to ask of you." She turned to look him in the eye. He was farther down the hill from her and she could now look him directly in the eyes. "I need a gun."

"Why do you need a gun?" Colin quickly questioned.

She quickly lifted the left side of her shirt to show him the mending bite mark. "I want to learn to shoot. I know some basics... my dad tried to teach me. I don't want Ashley or my parents to know about it."

"Why? Is there something you are not telling me, Em?" Colin questioned with disbelief.

Emily could see the shock on his face. She had spoken often about her dislike of guns.

"I refuse to be a victim. The animal is still out there. I know the likelihood of me seeing it again or being attacked is astronomical, but I am the only person this thing has attacked and lived. Do I really need to say anymore?" She did not let him say another word. Checking both directions, she rushed across the road on her way back to Colin's SUV.

———●———

EMILY SMILED FEELING the blistering hot water on her skin. The water rushed over her face and down her body—soap residue and sweat swirling down the drain—it ran through her soapy hair. She could not remember the last time she'd even washed it, but it felt like weeks had passed without the required attention her curly mane demanded. Her skin screamed with each spray of water for more. A feeling of being rejuvenated rushed over her. This was the next step in her renewal after being released from the hospital.

Emily paused for one last moment; the water swarmed her face just as she reached to turn the shower off. She stepped out onto the tile, hardly feeling the cold touch of the ceramic. Opening the door to the bathroom, she glanced to be sure the door to her bedroom was still closed before walking to the dresser. She slipped into a matching bra and panty set before pulling on pajama pants—similar to the ones she wore home, but red—a heavy, gray, zipped-down sweatshirt. She glanced in the mirror. Her hair—still wet—lay on her shoulders and across her face. With one last smile at her reflection, she walked to the door.

The smell smacked Emily in the face the moment she stepped into the room, and the sound coming from the kitchen was almost too loud to believe she had not heard it from the shower. She smiled stepping up to the counter just as Colin stood to mess with the skillet.

"Chicken stir-fry, salad, and…" there was a pause as he set the bottle of water in front of her, "water."

She returned his large smile taking the bottle in hand.

"Protein and veggies, a good welcome home meal."

"How domestic." She laughed, twisting the lid and taking a drink. It was cold and she could feel it all the way down her throat. Her skin was still red from the hot shower and she felt warmer with the sweatshirt.

"I do love to cook when it is called for," he replied, stirring with a wooden spoon. His back was to her. Her eyes drifted down his backside, but she could see little for the loose jeans and the too-large flannel shirt. "And I figure Ashley will only bring you pizza or some god awful take out. A home cooked meal was in order."

"Thank you…for everything," Emily said, snapping back to attention to look at the salad bowl within arm's reach. "When did you have time to go get all of this?" She reached into the bowl, grabbed a small blushing tomato, and placed it between her lips chewing. Without meaning to the juice spit to the counter and ran down her lip, she reached to clean it from her chin.

"Messy," Colin said, handing her a napkin.

"Shush." She finished cleaning her face and then the counter. "You planned this meal didn't you? Had it in a cooler in the truck? Don't lie!"

"Ashley asked me early this morning if I would give you a ride home from the hospital, so yeah I planned this," Colin said, turning and leaning against the counter. "I planned on getting you all liquored up and having my way with you. I just…well, forgot the liquor." He smiled his big boyish smile.

"Thank you." She reached for the bowl only to have her hand gently slapped.

"Wait for the rest," he said with a much more playful smile than the other one.

She replied with a wrinkle of her nose. "Have you thought about what I asked you earlier," Emily questioned, slouching in her seat with her hands now in the pocket of her sweatshirt.

"I have a Glock 9 millimeter I will loan you for the time being. I'll show you how to shoot." Colin turned away from her to attend the stir-fry. "We'll go see Mathew Bradley first. I don't know why you want to see him though. Dad told me stories…he is just a crazy old man."

"A crazy old man who saved my life," Emily replied, staring at the counter in front of her. "I want to thank him…and I have to know if he saw anything."

"He told the authorities he didn't see it, why would he lie?"

"Maybe he didn't see it…but if he did I will know."

"How?"

"I just will." She turned in her stool and stepped away from the counter.

"Colin…what is the closest you've ever come to dying?" Emily questioned. She had finally taken her seat in the living room on the couch, her bare feet propped underneath her.

"Motorcycle accident my senior year," he replied, never looking toward her as he finished preparations on the stir-fry.

"I remember that…you and that blond freshman cheerleader…" Emily said with a smile. "You were showing off. Which was it, the accident, or the confrontation with her father?"

Colin laughed. "I was lucky. She came away from the accident with only some scratched knees."

"Ah, so you only prepared her for future times with rough scratchy knees…" There was a long pause before she laughed.

"You know she was a sweet girl. I ran into her a few weeks back too," Colin said. He circled the counter with a plate and bowl in hand sitting them down in front of her. The bowl was the salad; the small plate was covered in almost as many fried veggies with a mixture of chicken. "Eat," he ordered leaving only to return a moment later with a bottle of dressing he sat beside the salad.

His last trip he had his own plate of stir-fry, but no salad. He took a seat on the couch opposite of Emily.

"Tasty." She finished off a third bite of the stir-fry. She had picked at it and mostly only eaten the chicken and broccoli.

"Eat all of it," Colin said with a big grin.

"I'm only going to let you get by with ordering me for so long, you know that right?" She grinned taking her next bite.

"Why did you ask, about the closest I have come to dying?" Colin questioned after a drink of water.

"You spent what—two days in the hospital? Several broken bones. Did you have nightmares?" Emily asked.

"Not that I can remember," Colin answered.

Emily did not try to change the subject she just did not speak as she concentrated on the food in front of her. "Really good."

"Thank you," Colin replied sitting back in his chair staring unblinking at his friend. "Do you want to talk about it?"

She had just poured the dressing on her salad and paused to look at him.

"I am a good listener."

"So, everyone keeps saying, but to be honest…I don't want to talk about it," Emily stated.

"Then why are we going to Bradley's tomorrow?"

"It's nothing, really…I just want to thank him," she replied.

They continued their meal in silence. Nearly fifteen minutes later, as they cleaned the dishes side-by-side, they spoke again.

"You don't have to worry about me Colin." She turned to face him.

"I do—we all do—after what happened to you," Colin stated, drying his hands off and turning to face her.

Emily stepped toward Colin and with ease moved him back into the corner of the cabinets. The same corner Troy had backed her into days before. She rose up and softly kissed him on the lips. As he started to speak, she set a finger to his mouth. She grabbed his flannel shirt with both hands and kissed him again. She pulled him into her, at the same time taking several steps back to keep him at her pace. She led him across the living room, through the bedroom door, and to the edge of the bed. Emily pulled at his shirt, snapping away the last two buttons she'd yet to loosen. Their lips had hardly left each other as they came to the bed from the kitchen. Her hands ran up his stomach, across his bare chest and then down his arms until they paused on his wrists. She pulled his hands close to her side as they rested on the top of her flannel pants.

They continued to kiss as she pulled the zipper of her sweatshirt until the thick material fell free, exposing her black lace bra. Again, her hands found his wrists and pulled them up from her pants to her bare waist and across the wound.

"We shouldn't…" He finally broke from her lips and was able to speak.

"We should," she replied pulling him into her.

She could feel his hands on her bare back now as they inched toward the clasp of her bra. The material stretched for only a moment before she allowed it to slide down her arms. She pressed against him and snapped her hands around his neck, playing with his curly blond hair before pulling his face down to her chest. She felt the soft touch of his lips on her breasts, his tongue circling her nipple causing her to breath heavier and faster. She pulled him tight against her as she stepped back into the bed and they both fell on the comforter. Moving her hands across his lower back and around to the front of his jeans she fought with the button until it released and then the zipper. She pushed his boxer briefs and pants down his thighs, stopping at his knees. She dug her fingernails in the flesh of his small back as his lips kissed her neck. She moaned. His lips on her neck, she moaned just as she felt the graze of his teeth on the soft skin. She pressed against him, his hand on the small of her back as he pulled her pajama pants down her legs and tossed them to the floor.

Colin stood and looked over her for a moment.

"Don't over think this." Emily sat up on the edge of the bed reaching to pull him closer.

She saw him smile his goofy smile as he stepped closer, kissing her on the forehead. She knew what was about to happen when he glanced at the wide-open door behind them.

"I can't do this…"

"Yes, you can." She could see he was more than able and interested in what was happening between them. She could not stop her eyes from roaming up and down his nearly naked lean body. Her nails slowly traced up and down his chest. She was daring herself to force him. She knew it wouldn't take much.

"No."

She watched as he stepped away from the bed. Without saying another word, he pulled his pants on and left the room. She stared in disbelief. She grabbed the sweatshirt as she ran from the room and was just pulling it on as he opened the door.

"Colin, wait…"

He stopped, looking back at her.

"Can we talk about this?" she questioned.

"I'll be by around one tomorrow," he answered. "We'll go by the Bradley's." He said nothing else, leaving her standing in the door wearing nothing but a half-zipped sweatshirt and panties. Emily had just reached the door when she saw Ashley's small car pull into the drive. As Colin got into his Blazer, Emily turned and walked back to her room.

◆

EMILY STEPPED BACK into the living room wearing her sleeping pants and a fully zipped sweatshirt just as Ashley entered the house. The first words out of her mouth were, "Why was Colin shirtless?" She was still looking out at the driveway as he sped off.

"It's nothing," Emily stated as she sat and watched her friend shut the door. "There is stir-fry and salad if you want some."

"You look flushed. How're you feeling?" Ashley questioned. The shorter woman was across the room in almost a flash, with her hand to Emily's forehead.

"Just tired," Emily replied trying to hide her frustration with a smile. "How was your date?" Emily moved away when Ashley removed her hand.

"It wasn't a date…just a getting to know you lunch." Ashley blushed.

Emily smiled. She could never remember seeing her friend blush before. She had, on occasion, turned red from embarrassment, but never a blush. "You like her, don't you?" Emily smiled.

"She's different," Ashley replied.

"You're blushing…and floating…"

Her friend glowed and stood with such ease as if the air itself was lifting her upward in her happiness.

"You must tell me all about this so-called *'getting to know you lunch'*."

9

EMILY LEANED OVER the butterscotch flavored coffee as the steam floated up into her face, taking in every breath of the fresh scent. She wore a dark maroon-colored long-sleeve shirt—a white t-shirt peeking out from underneath—with black jeans and long knee-high combat boots. It was still hours before Colin was due to arrive, but she was ready. Many things ran through her mind, from the long bloody dream she had in the hospital to the day before with Colin. She was glad now he'd stopped them from going any farther—no matter how badly she lusted after him. It was a reaction to the dream and everything that had happened to her, and not motivated by her own feelings or attraction to her friend. She wore little make-up…outside of lip-gloss, blush, and a hint of maroon eyeliner. Her dark-red hair—half pulled back from her face with a black hair band—hung over her shoulder in a wild unmanageable tangle.

The door to the bathroom opened and Ashley stumbled out and back to the couch where she crashed and almost instantly pulled the pillow overhead. "What time is it?"

"Eleven," Emily replied to the muffled question watching as dark locks of hair peeked out from the front of the pillow just before Ashley sat up. "You look like hell," she said as she took a sip of her coffee.

"Thank you, always love hearing that. Does wonders for my self-esteem," Ashley said as she stood up. She wore a simple t-shirt and gray shorts. She walked to the counter and sat down across from her friend. She pulled the coffee to her lips without even asking.

Emily only smiled as she sipped. "Stay up, late did you?"

"Was channel surfing until sometime after five," she replied.

"You were watching over me, weren't you?"

"Yes," Ashley replied before taking another sip of coffee. "Where do you think you are going anyways?"

"Colin is coming by to pick me up…going to get some fresh air…get out of a bed for a day before I go crazy," Emily replied.

"Short trip."

"Maybe." Emily took the offered coffee cup and took a drink of her own. "What are your plans today?"

"I have to go to work," Ashley replied.

Her friend never spent a lot of time in school but what she lacked in educational ambition she made up for by holding down full-time jobs—currently as a bartender at a redneck country bar and grill. She hated her job and everything that came with it, but the tips were good and she was capable of managing her own hours.

"Any dreams last night?"

"I don't even remember lying down," Emily replied truthfully. She had so much on her mind when she did lay down it was right to sleep. A peaceful night's slumber until seven and she had been up drinking coffee since.

"Colin going to stick around until I get in tonight?" Ashley questioned.

"I won't be alone any today. Promise." Emily smiled.

Emily tried not to look at him and the drive was filled with only meaningless chatter. Each time she glanced at him, she could see images of him without his shirt on. It caused her heart to race and she swore she could smell his skin. Colin kept his attention mostly on the road in front of them as they traveled what seemed like half a day. They journeyed through back roads and one lane hollows until he brought his truck to a stop in front of an old wooden gate. Colin had told her when he picked her up he had already drove by Mathew Bradley's home where his son had told him he was at the family cabin. Colin had only been there once as a teenager but knew the way.

Emily never questioned why Colin had attempted to pay the man a visit without her—even if it was on her mind. The tension was there between them and he kept his distance from her at all times. Though she tried to do the same, her eyes continued to wander and get lost on him.

"Looks like we are walking." He stepped away from the gate. A doubled chain and padlock gleamed in the afternoon sun. The air was cold and the weatherman had said the temperature would be lucky to top fifty-five at the height of the day. She kept her black jacket and hands in her pocket as they circled around the front of the gate.

"How far?" she questioned. Colin had waited to make sure she made it clear around the edge before he started to walk.

"Two miles, steady uphill," he replied. Colin was not as bundled against the cold as she—he wore a pullover black t-shirt with a long-sleeve white thermal shirt underneath, jeans and boots—but he showed no sign of being cold. She was several steps behind him and could see the bulge at the small of his back under the shirt.

"You're packing?" she questioned.

He turned and walked several paces backward. "It's the 9mm you said you wanted. After we are done here I'll take you by the range."

"Thank you," she replied.

•

THEY WERE A mile and a half into the walk when Colin's pace slowed and he became more attentive to their surroundings.

"Should I be worried about this guy?" she questioned.

"You were raised around here just like me," Colin replied. He watched both sides of the road every noise causing him to turn to check behind them. "Some people don't like company. There is a reason all of these older folk have their cabins and such—some with no technology—a place to get away from people. So, visitors aren't always welcome."

"I can see that." Emily paused in her tracks and Colin immediately saw why she stopped.

A large slab cut from an oak stump hung on a post next to the road. Words had been meticulously carved into the surface, sealed for longevity with a heavy coat of varnish that glistened in the sun. It was obvious a lot of work had gone into making the sign, which read simply: "*Trespassers will be shot withut warnin and buried in a deep dark hole*".

"Too late to turn back now." Colin smiled. "Don't worry; I think he will warn us first."

After another hundred feet, they rounded a long curve and could see the cabin a mere couple hundred yards farther away. Emily stopped in her tracks to take in the property before her. The cabin was of rough lumber and supported a classic barn-red metal roof. Smoke bellowed from a stove pipe. There was no porch, just a big wooden door that sat directly in the middle of the home. It was surrounded on either side by the only two visible windows at the front of the cabin. To the right of the door was a large stack of cut firewood and buckets that—she could only assume from this distance—were filled with coal. A nearly new Dodge truck was parked nearby, its thick tires had cut deep ruts into the road before them.

"Shouldn't we try to make our presence known before we get too close?" Emily questioned.

Colin only laughed as he began to walk.

"What is so funny?"

Colin stopped laughing and turned on her. "What do you propose we try? Throwing rocks at his windows? Shooting off the pistol? I think it's best we walk right up to the front door and knock."

Emily stopped in her tracks, stunned by his tone and coldness as he continued to walk. She'd known Colin since they were teenagers and he had never snapped at her as coldly as he had. "Don't be mean," she mumbled. Unsure if he had even heard—she hoped he hadn't—she picked up her pace to catch him.

They were still several yards from the cabin when a low growl startled them both. The growl escalated into a yodeling-howl of warning as a hound charged around the opposite side of the cabin. The old dog stopped several steps away but continued to bark and snarl, being sure to show off its teeth—many of which were missing.

"I think he'll know we are here soon." Colin looked back at Emily several steps away from him.

The dog looked directly at her and it caused her to shiver. She wrapped her arms across her chest and on instinct took a step away from the dog. The animal responded by taking two steps toward her.

A man circled around the front of the Dodge at their back. Emily jumped at his sudden appearance, noticing the shotgun in his arms. The weapon was camouflage—just like his brimmed hat, long jacket, and overalls. Even his boots were camo.

"Worst thing you can do, little missy, is show fear," he said, the sound of his voice ceased the dogs barking and it backed away without making another sound.

The first thing Emily saw was the shotgun in his arms—full camouflage, much like the clothing he wore. He wore a brimmed hat, a long jacket that stretched down past his hips and overalls—she could see the strap as they hung at his side. Even his boots, were of the same camouflage break pattern. "Showin' fear to an ol' dog means you done lost and he won." His voice was kind with a bit of a hoarse tone from age.

He was thin, with a lean face that only enhanced his most noticeable feature, his mustache. It circled down past the corner of his lips, then back up in a half-twirl—and was as white as winter's snow. The rest of his face was clean-shaven and rough from age. Thick, bushy eyebrows covered his thin, dark eyes—eyes that were taking a long hard look at Emily. "You're looking much spryer than last I saw."

Emily let out a half laugh, exhaling with relief as she smiled. Her arms were now down and relaxed, but she could not shake the startle the dog had given her.

"And you" the old man said, turning to Colin, "are looking different from the last I saw you. Dwight's boy all grown up—you look more like your father now. You two are friends?" He motioned between them.

"Yes sir," Colin replied.

"You know how lucky your friend is to be standing here today, young man?" the man stated, taking the shotgun out of his arms and leaning it against the thick tread of the tires. "Turn around let me look at you, missy."

Emily turned completely around before she again faced him.

"I see she follows directions—does she speak?" He looked to Colin.

"I'm sorry," Emily muttered with a half-smile, still shaking.

"Nothing to be sorry for. You are up and walking around," he replied. "You were in pretty rough shape the last I saw you, little lady. So tell me why did you come all this way to see an old man?"

"I wanted to know about that night..." Emily paused looking at Colin and then back to the old man. The look of a gentle old man was gone, replaced with fear of the question he was asked. His composure changed—as if the man was about to collapse from having the wind knocked from him.

Emily wasn't the only one to notice.

"Mr. Bradley, are you alright?" Colin questioned.

She knew immediately the story told to the nurses at the hospital the night of her attack wasn't the entire story.

"I'm fine." He broke his gaze on Emily and looked to Colin. "You will know one of these days when you are as old as me, I just need to take a seat." He picked up his shotgun and walked past them.

"Here, let me help." Colin stepped up beside him and the old man stopped in his tracks.

"The pretty girl can humor me with her help, but you don't mind giving us a moment or two to talk, do you, Dwight?"

Colin took a step back, not bothering to correct the old man when he called him by his father's name.

Emily took the old man by the hand but could tell he did not need help as they entered the cabin. She paused inside the door looking back at Colin—whose back was now to her—as he looked off toward the woods. Then she saw the old hound, only a couple steps behind, keeping an eye on her—his quivering lip still showing his aged teeth. The very presence of the dog caused her to take a couple of clumsy steps into the cabin.

"Shut the door," Bradley said. Emily shifted her nervous gaze from the dog to Bradley and shut the door. As she turned, she noticed the armory in the living room—that also doubled as a dining room and possibly the bedroom of the cabin. The table was covered with ammunition—a couple of rifles and three handguns. She turned as she felt him step closer to her.

"Have you a snort." Bradley handed a glass to her.

Emily lifted the glass to her lips, not even bothering to inquire what the questionable drink was. The bitter tasting liquid burned all the way down, but she didn't cough.

"An experienced drinker." He smiled, taking the glass and returning it to the small kitchen area.

A stove, a fridge, and a couple of big fridge-sized cabinets took up most of the room. The kitchen was separated from the other room only by a bar styled counter very similar to the one in her own home.

"I have had my share." Emily turned to look at the living area. A couch pulled out as a bed, covers and pillows were scattered about and several duffle bags of clothing and other accessories were strewn around the room.

"I bet, young lady."

She smiled at the irony of the conversation being about her experience in the consumption of alcohol, yet he still called her 'lady'.

Emily saw yet another handgun as it peeked out from under the pillow on the makeshift bed. She turned to look behind her. It was hidden by the door, but there sat a shotgun and a large machete.

"Another?" Bradley asked.

She turned as he stepped back into the room. She showed no hesitation as she took the glass, and in unison, they both drank down their shots. She handed back her glass and returned his smile.

"So you are here because you want to know what an old man saw."

"You did see it, didn't you?" Emily watched him return to the counter and begin to pour a couple more shots.

"To be honest, sweetheart, I don't know what I saw that night," he replied with a glance back over his shoulder. "I almost didn't see you there in the road." He took another drink of his own before he refilled both their glasses and approached her. "I wasn't driving fast or anything of the sort when I came into those curves, but see…my judgment may have been slightly obscured." Bradley lifted his glass into the air with a smile. "What happened in that last curve was enough to sober up the drunkest sailor on leave." He finished off his drink and watched as Emily did the same.

Bradley took both glasses back to the sink but did not refill them. He walked past her taking a seat at the table. "I never actually saw the animal, miss. It was more of a feeling as I came out of that last curve—somethin' kept my attention off the road and drew it to the embankment where you wrecked. The truth is I never even saw your car until after I picked your broken body up from the pavement. I only saw shadows. I was nearly on top of you before I saw you there—swerved to miss and was several car lengths past before I even realized you weren't some deer carcass."

Emily was shocked by his account of the events.

"Somethin' about that night, in that moment…I almost couldn't make myself get out of the truck. I was startled but it was more than just about hitting you—somethin' inside scared me shitless. I backed my truck up and opened the door for only a moment before I closed it and locked it. I remember my daddy telling me stories of the war and fear—in those moments when you grow numb and you just don't know how to deal. I saw war myself. I saw war, myself. I saw things back in my day that would scare the hell out of most, but none of those memories give me the feeling I got that night. That moment, all I could see was darkness—but you just know somethin' isn't right. Somethin' is there…waiting to get you."

Emily knew the feeling. She could remember it well from that night, knowing there was something out there she just could not see.

"I scooted across the seat. I wasn't outside of the truck…a handful of seconds. I scooped you off the ground and put you in the truck. Even bumped your head on the door in the process. I never looked at your wounds—you were covered in mud, blood and who knows what else. I just knew I had to get you out of there. Even over the roar of my engine, I heard it in the darkness—the intense hate filled growl. It was like no dog's growl I'd ever heard. I pulled the door shut and locked it, crawled over top of you back to my seat, I couldn't get out of there fast enough. You just kept muttering for God to help you, dear."

"I'm thankful you were there." Emily moved from her position just inside the door of the cabin. For the first time she saw the papers at her feet—scattered and opened—they were all about the attacks.

"That's not all…" the old man looked ashamed to finish.

Emily could see him shake and the fear set in on his face.

"As I drove, I saw somethin' in my rearview. It was mostly just a shadow but at the very spot where you had lain. As tall as any man, it stood and stretched and—I swear I was a mile away, music on…the sound of your wounded breathing and mumbling, my own heart—I still heard it howl out in anger over a missed meal."

Emily had lost all color in her appearance and was as shaken as Bradley over the description of what he had seen—even in the dark of night in his drunken haze. She remembered the eyes as they looked into her own back glass at her…as if it had lowered to just look in.

"I do not know what I truly saw that night. Part of me thinks the liquor was playin' with my mind…but I remember it as if I were as sober as the day my momma had me. I could not tell the police or the game enforcement about that—I would still be locked in the box. That is the honest truth of what I saw, just between you and me."

"I understand," Emily stated.

"I have seen in the paper, more deaths since that night and not a single survivor…you realize how lucky you are?" Mathew Bradley asked.

"So I have been told a number of times." Emily paused, as she tried to catch her breath. "I could really use another drink."

Bradley smiled, walked to the kitchen area and got them both another shot.

<hr>

THE DOOR TO the cabin crept open and Emily stepped out. Colin was seated beside the Dodge truck, but it was the waiting hound that greeted her. Its lip quivered on the edge of a growl.

"Down boy," Bradley said stepping out of the door. The dog looked to its master before running past Emily and into the cabin.

"Thank you, Mr. Bradley," Emily replied, turning but continuing to move away from the cabin.

"I wish you the best, young Emily. You take care of yourself… watch those shadows," he stated shutting the door. No doubt, he was going back for another drink.

"I was beginning to worry," Colin said as she approached.

"I lost track of time," Emily replied looking at her watch and realizing almost an hour had passed since she entered the cabin.

"It will be dark soon—don't think we'll have time to shoot today," Colin said.

Emily had already walked past him at an almost fevered pace down the road. "I know. I would really like to get back to your truck before dark," she replied.

It did not take long before they reached his SUV, but the shadows were beginning to grow as he unlocked the door. The walk was a fast one. At times, Emily almost seemed to break into a jog and Colin struggled to keep up. She released a breath of relief as she buckled her seat belt and looked at Colin in the driver's seat.

"What did he tell you? Did he see the animal?"

"No," she quickly replied. "It was just like you heard at the hospital." She knew she could not tell Colin about the large animal Bradley had seen in the shadow howling in the moonlight. Not about the ramblings of an old drunk—even when she knew what he said was true. She may not have seen the animal but she knew it was true.

MUCH LIKE THE drive to Bradley's the return trip consisted of random chit-chat between Emily and Colin, but for the most part they were silent. They pulled into the drive. Ashley's vehicle was there and the lights in the living room were on. Emily got out of the vehicle and quickly moved to the front door and into her home.

She did not expect to find a gathering inside. The smell of fresh food filled the room. She stepped around the counter to see her friend, Ashley, the nurse Lauren and her parents all in the kitchen. She turned immediately to Colin, who had stepped up behind her.

"I had no idea—promise." He removed his jacket and placed it on the arm of the nearest couch.

Emily entered the kitchen to find her father standing behind her usual seat at the dining table. A plate of steamed vegetables and sliced pork roast graced her place-setting.

"What is this?" Emily questioned. This was only the second time since she moved into the house her parents had been there. She did not recall seeing their car outside in the drive.

"It's a we-are-all-ecstatic-you-are-alright dinner," Ashley said. She was seated in the closest chair on the left, right next to where Emily's father stood waiting for her to take a seat. Her hair was different from this morning—streaks of red and pink mixed with her black tangles. She held a long-stem wine glass in her hand. To her left was Lauren—who sat in silence—but looked at Emily objectively. The other end of the table was empty; though a plate was there. She caught a glimpse of Colin as he walked around to take the seat. He had to have known, despite what he told her. To the right side of the table, in the farthest chair, her mom sat with a large smile. The closest chair to her was empty, waiting for her father to retake his seat.

"You shouldn't have done this," Emily stated. There was a moment of silence as each of the guests looked at one another.

"Might as well get past it. We are worried about you," Ashley piped in before anyone else could break the silence.

There was a momentary glare between the woman and Emily's father. Emily took her seat and watched as her father returned to his.

"I'm fine," Emily replied. She was re-running her conversation with Mathew Bradley in her mind—the story he'd told her of what he remembered from the night of the attack. The description of what he heard, of what he saw in the road…it was all replaying in front of her. The more she thought about it, the more it hurt—in the back of her skull, even in her eyes. Everything seemed to throb. The beginning of a headache. She glanced at everyone at the table…her friends, family and a woman she had only just met.

"You say that," her mom said.

"The doctor said I was fine as well," she replied quickly. "He said with the latest tests there was no reason I couldn't return to normal, everyday life."

"Don't get snippy," her dad called out.

Emily looked back-and-forth from her parents to her friends, but none of them looked at her, with the exception of Ashley. The other woman's hand was on the table; her flashy purple fingernails were closer to her own wrist than before.

"Sorry I think I'm getting a headache," she replied with an apologetic smile and expression toward her mother. She then felt her father's hand on her forehead.

"You're not running a temperature," he stated.

Her view of everyone was blocked by his forearm. As he pulled his hand away, and she could once again see everyone around the table, she gasped—almost out loud with horror, at what she saw. She quickly closed her eyes and reopened them. What was only a moment of darkness seemed like minutes to her. Was she dreaming? She had seen all of them with a variety of attack injuries. But now everything was normal. She looked at each of those around the table and then back to her father. "I think I need to lie down. May I be excused?" She waited for his nod before getting up and leaving the table.

———————●———————

EMILY SHUT THE door behind her as she entered the bedroom. She leaned against the door even pushed against the wooden structure. It was a hallucination…a nightmare—while she was wide-awake. She could still taste the bile in her throat as she tried to swallow. Her heart raced as the image of everyone who cared about her with their throats torn out and faces shredded by claws engraved in her mind. Dr. Knox said this might happen—dreams while she was wide-awake.

Before she could even move from the door there came a soft knock. "Emily."

She turned and opened the door just enough for Ashley to slip in and again she shut it.

"I had no idea they were going to come by," she quickly stated.

"I believe you. This was my father's doing," she replied. She tried to hide the fact that she was on the verge of a panic attack, but as she took a deeper and deeper breath her heaving chest gave her away. "I thought you were going to work tonight?"

"I called in once your parents showed. I couldn't leave you alone with them this evening," Ashley stated.

Emily crossed the room and sat on the bed before she rolled over with her still muddy boots just off the side. She said nothing as the other woman took a seat at the end of the bed and began to take her boots off. One-by-one, she tossed the boots to the floor and then pulled her socks off. "You look flushed, same type of ache as last night?"

"Huh?" she questioned, remembering when Ashley had gotten home the night before. "Oh, no, was just exhausted last night."

"And now? Full blown headache?"

Emily twisted to place her legs over the bed and rolled to her side in an almost fetal position.

"Have you taken anything today?"

"No." Emily had forgotten all about her medication.

Ashley stood from the bed and left the bedroom, returning only a moment later with a cup and pills in hand. She handed them over.

Emily quickly took them. "Are they mad?"

"They are eating." Ashley took a seat just as Emily curled back into a comfortable position.

"You should go eat too," Emily replied.

"Truthfully, I'm not all that hungry or interested," Ashley said.

"Did you and Lauren have plans?" Emily questioned.

"We were going to get a drink after work. She showed up shortly after your parents did," she responded with a smile. "I think I like this one."

"I can tell," Emily replied with a smile. Her headache was getting worse but she tried to hide it. At least her breathing had returned to normal.

"Don't change the subject now—how bad is it? Do you need to go to the doctor?" Ashley questioned.

"Just need to close my eyes," she replied.

"Okay, I'll check on you in a bit," Ashley replied, getting up from the bed and leaving the room.

Emily barely made it under the covers before she fell fast asleep.

10

EMILY ROLLED OVER. She was still in her clothes from the day before. A quick glance at the clock, she had slept most of the evening away. Slowly standing she could see light coming in from the living room. She crept to the bathroom, quickly changing into a pair of sleeping pants and her old worn t-shirt, before returning to the bedroom. She started to crawl into bed but the low rumble of her stomach stopped her. She knew there were leftovers from the meal somewhere in the kitchen.

Emily stepped into the living room and saw that Ashley was fast asleep on the couch. She crossed the living room, turning the light off in the process. It was then she saw the other woman. Lauren sat at the counter, laptop in front of her and half-filled wine glass at her side. She gave a half wave, "Are you feeling better?"

"Much," Emily replied, looking in the Frigidaire, and finding a plate full of food covered and waiting. She pulled it out, crossed to the microwave, and began to heat the meal.

"Let me look at you."

Emily turned to see the other woman was at her side and almost as suddenly, she was looking directly into her eyes. She wanted to push her away but knew if she did, it might wake Ashley. She also knew she only had her best interests in mind.

"Pupils are normal. No temperature. So, the headache is gone?"

"All gone, only hungry now," she smiled, as the beep of the microwave cut in. "Ashley asked you to stay?"

"I offered. I could see how worried she was about you. I hope you don't mind." Lauren crossed back to the other side of the counter.

"Not at all. I kind of expected you'd stick around. How long did my parents stay?" Emily questioned.

"Colin left not long after you went to bed. Your parents stayed until a few hours ago," Lauren stated shifting in her seat to watch both her laptop screen and Emily.

Lauren looked from her to Ashley across the room almost as if to make sure she was asleep, and then back to Emily.

"What?" Emily smiled before she took a drink of water.

"Ashley and your parents—more to the point Ashley and your dad…there seems to be some ill feelings there?" Lauren questioned, shutting laptop, pulling the wine glass around in front of her.

Emily smiled just before she took another bite. "I've known Ashley since freshman year of high school. So, going on ten years now," Emily replied before she took another drink of water. "With Ash, what you see now is just an older more developed version of what she was freshman year. Full of attitude and takes shit from no one, teachers, parents, other students it did not matter. I was a jock, I played softball, volleyball, lacrosse, ran track and I hung out with the popular kids. We did not get along. Everyone talked about her—the new kid when so many of us knew each other from middle school and farther back. I was one of those. One night at a party, I had a little too much to drink and a senior boy, Jeremy Jackson, was getting a little friendlier than I wanted. I don't even know who invited Ashley; she may have just crashed the party. Either way she toppled him rather violently. From then on, no one talked about her…at least in any way it could get back to her. We really weren't friends, even then. First day of sophomore year we had a number of classes together…and from there we have been friends ever since. She was out by then, I was going through a lot of personal things at home and felt like an outcast even though I still associated with the popular kids. We bonded, over home issues. The first time I introduced her and my father, her hair was like fourteen different colors, she was wearing ripped-up punk clothing, piercings, and even a few fake tattoos…my father disapproved from the start. I don't think either of them has ever truly tried to get along with the other, they have just tolerated each other for me."

"She is spunky. It's nice to know she has always been that way," Lauren stated.

"So," there was a long pause as Emily looked from her plate to Lauren and smiled. "Tell me about Lauren?"

"Is this where you check-up on who your friend is dating?" Lauren questioned with a smile.

"To be honest, Ash has never had the best of luck with who she chooses to date…maybe as bad as me." They both looked at the woman across the room who still appeared to be sleeping.

"I'm twenty-eight. I spend most of my time at the hospital—it takes up the majority of my time actually. Not much of a social life," Lauren replied.

"What about when you do have free time, what do you like to do?" Emily questioned.

"I'm a big reader, I enjoy movies…I like to go for long hikes," she replied.

Emily smiled big as she looked down.

Lauren noticed. "What is it?"

"Ash is not a big reader and hates the outdoors…she'd rather go to a concert than a movie." Emily smiled. She covered her food back up. "I think I'm going to try and get some sleep. I'm glad you came tonight."

Lauren only nodded as she went back to what she was doing before.

Emily crawled under her covers, staring at the ceiling above. She smiled. She was happy her friend had found someone, even if they were different. She knew Lauren was good for her.

EMILY FOUND HERSELF alone the next morning, both Ashley and Lauren having gone their respective ways. It was near noon when Emily emerged from the house to check the mailbox, still in her sleeping ware and hair pulled back into a ponytail with no makeup on her face. She was halfway down the driveway when she saw the truck—or more importantly the man leaning against the large Suburban. "Ms. Emily Meyer?" the man questioned.

"You already know I am." Emily stopped in her tracks. The man was in his mid-to-late thirties, his short messy hair was the only thing about him out of place. His eyes were blue, and even from the distance they stood out. The kind of blue people used to describe the sky or the ocean. His face was clean-shaven and he wore a sleek black suit, with shined shoes. The suit seemed to hug him at every joint and muscle. She did not know for sure, but he seemed like a man in very good physical shape. More than just a runner—this man spent time in a gym. A lot of time. He unbuttoned his jacket placing his hands on his side revealing the holster on his belt. Instinctively, Emily took a step back and even glanced to the door of her home.

"Detective Rodney Hastings." He smiled.

It was the smile of a man who knew more than he should about a person just by looking at them, she thought. His smile made him all the more attractive.

Emily never saw the woman until she came around the back of the Suburban. She wore her short black hair in a pixie cut. Her suit was similar to Hastings's—black and sleek, unbuttoned to show the freshly ironed, white shirt underneath. She even had a similar gun holster. She was thin with a straight figure and if not for the way the pants hung to her thighs, she could have almost passed as a 'twig'. Even though she was a woman with near zero curves, she was likely as fit as Hastings. The sleeves of her jacket were rolled up exposing her forearms. Emily could see they were thin but muscular.

"This is Rebecca Vance, we were wondering if we could ask you a few questions."

"About?" Emily crossed her arms under her bust.

"Troy Anders," Hastings replied.

"What about him?" Emily quickly asked. She never wanted to hear the man's name again.

"We were wondering when the last time you saw him was?" Hastings spoke again; his voice was gruff with a hint of humor in each word. His partner was at the back of the Suburban and stood in a similar position as Emily. She could tell little about the woman who wore thick sunglasses over her eyes, but it looked like she wore next to no make-up besides lip-gloss.

"It has been a few days," Emily replied.

"Could you be more exact?" Vance asked in a harsh direct manner.

"October…28th, I think." She remembered it more clearly than she let on. It was the day she had the seizure that put her back in the hospital. Both of the detectives looked at one another and then back at her.

"You don't deny seeing him late that evening?" Vance inquired. There was no change in her tone.

"What is this about?" Emily dropped her hands to her sides and watched as the woman did the same. Emily no longer looked at the male detective but didn't take her eyes off the female detective. Going as far as to almost close her eyes in a glare of disapproval at the obvious mocking of her movements, but the woman showed no response.

"What was your relationship with Mr. Anders, if you don't mind us asking?" Hastings questioned.

Emily heard him but did not take her eyes off Vance. Her heart beat faster. She felt an internal struggle. There was something about the other woman she instantly did not like.

"I kind of do mind answering that," Emily replied.

"It would be in your best interest if you did," Vance stated, stepping up from the back of the Suburban to the sidewalk and placing a hand on her left hip, very close to the holstered weapon.

"We were lovers…"

"And the night of the 28th?" Hastings questioned. "Did you have relations on this particular night?"

"No…maybe…no," Emily replied still glaring at Vance angrily.

"Yes or no?" Vance questioned.

"What is this about?" Emily questioned.

"Troy Anders is dead Ms. Meyer."

It broke her glare on the other detective as she looked to Hastings, stumbling backward and almost falling to the pavement, but steadied herself.

"His body was found the morning of October the 29th. According to autopsy findings he was killed sometime late on the 28th. Almost all of the test results came back animal."

The growing anger, frustration, and disgust in her stomach made her feel on the edge of throwing up. She remembered the dream she had the morning she woke up in the hospital after the seizure, of an animal attacking Troy.

"On his face, scratches," Emily replied trying to regain her strength in her stance. "He was attacked by an animal?"

"Yes. How convenient the attack was after your own run-in with the animal terrorizing the rural area that your boyfriend would have a similar altercation but not live," Vance stated.

"He was no longer my boyfriend," Emily quickly replied.

"Obviously," Vance stated just as quickly.

"The two of you got physical, you don't deny that? Hastings questioned.

"No, I don't. We made out. We got physical and it became too intense and I scratched his face…then I had a seizure and spent three days in the hospital," Emily shot back, looking toward Hastings before again glaring at the female detective. She was angry; she could feel it as she shivered. It was more than anger. She was uncontrollably pissed… especially at the female detective. If they were pulling a good cop, bad cop, Detective Vance had bitch cop down.

"What time did he leave your home?" Hastings questioned.

"Shouldn't I have a lawyer present…?" Emily asked. She knew she did not kill Troy. Or at least, she thought she could not have killed him, but then there was the dream.

"Do you need one?" questioned Vance.

"I think I do."

"We just want to know what time he left your home." Hastings asked, and at that moment, Vance turned away from them to circle around to the other side of the Suburban and Hastings stepped toward her.

"Bitch," she said much louder than she meant to and it was obvious Hastings heard her as he approached with a smile.

"Do you remember what time it was?" He pulled out a card and handed it to her.

"Around six I think…it was just starting to get dark," she replied, taking the card from his hand.

"Thank you," he said with his sideways smile. "If you can think of anything we need to know about that night do not hesitate to call."

Emily shot a look over the man's shoulder to the other detective already in the passenger seat. She did not move until Hastings got into the driver's seat and the vehicle was gone.

OVER A DAY passed before Emily could even be convinced to leave the house again. She sat at an outside table with the umbrella opened above her. The air was brisk and chilly, and large gusts moved the umbrella unpredictably. Her hair was straightened; it was a change she was not convinced she wanted until after Ashley did it. Her long, flat, dark-red hair had a different shine to it straight that she'd never really noticed before. Large rimmed sunglasses covered her eyes—which were still red and puffy—as she tried to keep her sadness over the news of Troy's death hidden. She wore a netted black shirt over a black long-sleeve shirt in a lighter shade of black, with denim jeans and ankle-high black shoes.

Her cell phone sat in front of her, as well as a cup of hot tea. She would not lie, the tea tasted awful but it was therapeutic… though that did not change the after taste of each sip.

"May I?"

She looked up as Dr. Knox pulled the chair out. "I'm glad you called."

"I'm not sure why I did," Emily replied.

"Company maybe?" The woman motioned for a nearby waitress. "Coffee, black. Please." Knox was dressed very similar to the first time Emily remembered seeing her, in a black pinstriped suit and skirt. It was likely the same suit. "Are you still having dreams?"

"Not since I left the hospital a few days ago," Emily answered. "I met the guy who saved me that night."

"Did you get the answers you were hoping for?" Knox questioned.

"I'm not sure if they were the answers I was hoping for as much as he told me what I knew he would say." Emily took a slow sip of her tea.

"And how do you feel about the news of your former love?" Knox questioned. Emily looked at her with disbelief. She knew about Troy's death.

"Honestly...I hated him, but he didn't deserve what the detectives said happened. Can you believe a detective had the nerve to insinuate I had something to do with it? I know it was unlikely someone I know could be killed by this monster but I couldn't have done what they said," she replied. She was glad the doctor could not see the mix of anger and sadness through her glasses. She was having a difficult time holding back tears.

"Monster?" Knox asked, crossing her legs.

Everything about the older woman screamed therapist to Emily, even the way she sat in her uncomfortable metal chair. There was an ease about her that got people to open up to her. "What?"

"Before, you always called it animal or beast when I talked to you, but just now you called it a monster," Knox stated.

"Did I?" Emily replied, not realizing her slip. "You have to admit, it cannot be a normal animal, can it? I mean, it has killed so many now and the authorities can do nothing more than issue a curfew and warnings."

"I agree, it might not be a normal animal. Something is wrong with it. But calling it a monster?" Knox replied.

"I meant nothing like that," Emily replied with a smile. "Nothing crazy."

"Just a slip of the tongue then," Knox replied with a questioning glare. "Have you done anything…fun since you were released from the hospital?"

"What do you mean by fun?" Emily replied.

"I mean any kind of activity to maybe take your mind off of what happened. Be around new people, go to a theater, go dancing, just get out and be young and alive?" Knox asked. "Doctor's orders. Don't get too crazy with the drinking, but just get out of the house for the evening. I am sure your friend can help you with that."

"Thank you." Emily smiled. She stood to leave the table. It was then she saw him—a man across the street on a bench watching her. She could see little of him from the distance, but he was dressed completely in black. From his seated position, his long black coat almost reached the pavement below him. She knew on instinct, he watched her every move sending a chill up her body.

"Something wrong Emily?" Knox questioned.

"No, just thought I saw someone…I know." She quickly added the last part, glancing back to where she had seen him, but he was gone.

11

"I TAKE BACK everything I ever said about the doctor." Ashley called out from the other room. "They need to prescribe fun more often."

Emily forced a smile. She glared at her reflection in the mirror. She did not feel up to a night out on the town or being around crowds of people. Even the clothing she wore felt out of place, the dark green dress as it cut off just above her knees was happy and colorful—accentuated by two large brown belts, one to show off her bust the other below it to show her waist. Her knee-high, brown boots sported a four-inch heel and always made dancing an experience—though she was certain there would be no dancing tonight. A cross necklace hung from her neck though few would pay attention to the symbol, as it always seemed to get lost in her small cleavage.

"You're wearing that?" Ashley entered the room with a big smile. "You'll have all the guys using the old 'that dress will look good on my floor line' tonight."

Emily only smiled into the mirror at her friend as she finished applying dark eyeliner.

"I can't believe we are doing this," she muttered.

"What? Going out and having some much-needed fun with moderate drinking?" Ashley replied.

Her friend's hair was still as multicolored as the night before, but her attire was more casual. A black shirt ripped at the shoulder so it exposed them but the sleeves still hung to the arms, tight jeans over open-toed boots made a noticeable sound as she walked. Emily gave her a couple of glances before she returned to her own reflection.

"Is Lauren coming?" Emily questioned.

Ashley's smile instantly changed. "She is working tonight," she replied.

"So, are you two an item now?" she questioned.

"I don't know," she replied. "But enough about me and her…tonight is all about you."

Emily could tell there was something more; Ashley wasn't one to dodge questions about potential lovers. Something had gone wrong.

————————◆————————

THE CLUB WAS loud. Techno dance music bounced from wall to wall and the sound of people talking and having fun was almost as loud as the music. Emily sat in a booth, with Ashley at her left and another woman at the right. Kari was a friend—though more Ashley's—she knew from a previous job. It wasn't unusual for her to make up the third of the party when they had a girls' night out. Kari was thin and petite, even next to Ashley and Emily. Her raven-black hair only enhanced her pale complexion. A couple years younger, she often wore small thin-rimmed glasses over her green eyes. She wore several necklaces, a couple held tight against her throat and a couple more floated about her collarbone. She wore a black t-shirt advertising a local rock band, sleeveless to expose her thin muscular arms. A number of similar bracelets hung about her wrists similar in color to the tight necklaces, black fingerless gloves on her left hand, she wore often to hide a scar on the palm of her hand. A plaid skirt, that some would call provocative, in green-and-black plaid showed off her muscular legs even through the black netted stockings. Black combat boots finished off her ensemble, as they stretched not far from the knees.

"I'm going to get us some drinks," Ashley yelled out leaving the booth.

"I am so sorry I have not been by to see you. Up until yesterday, I was out of town," Kari whispered as she scooted closer to Emily. Emily was sure it was a lie.

"It is okay, the last thing I needed was another person looking over me," Emily quickly replied. Her hand was now entangled in the other woman's tight grip. She hated to say it, but she had not even noticed the absence of Kari since their friendship was mostly because of a mutual connection to Ashley.

Ashley returned with three bottles in hand. She set one down in front of each woman. The next song began and there was a glance between the two other women.

"Come on let's dance."

Emily felt the grip on each of their hands but she did not budge. "Go. I'm just going to enjoy the music." She watched as the other two left for the dance floor. Emily took another drink of her beer and leaned against the table wondering what she was doing here. Ashley and Kari could not have been gone more than a minute when the feeling of someone sitting beside her broke her from her lost daydreams.

"Hey there sexy? What are doing sitting alone?" The guy reeked of alcohol, sweat, and cheap cologne. His hair had enough grease in it for days and his opened shirt exposed a shaved chest.

"Go away," she said with a hollow tone.

"You say 'go away' but your body says come closer." He scooted closer to her. His hand sat on her forearm, even pressing down on hers trying to show his strength. She dragged her hand free from his, he again tried as she dug her nails into his palm, a moment later he pulled free, "bitch," he muttered as he left.

Ashley sat back down with a glare of evil intent for the man as he left, "Poser. Are you ok?' she questioned scooting over beside her.

"I'm fine." She glared at her blood-tipped fingernails. She had not meant to break the skin on his hand, but it felt so easy.

"We can leave if you want to," Ashley stated.

"We should stay, even if it is just to hear the music…and be out of the house." Emily looked to her friend with a big smile. "I don't mean to be a downer…I just don't feel like dancing."

"I understand. So, we shall drink, talk, and listen to music," Ashley said, as she tipped her beer at her friend for a toast.

"Where did you lose Kari?" Emily questioned. She noticed the other woman did not return.

"To some guy on the dance floor, and I saw the guy here, so, I thought I would come back and check on you," Ashley replied.

"I can take care of myself. I promise before I leave here with any guy he will meet your approval," Emily placed her hand on Ashley's free one, the blood still matted to the nails.

◆

NEARLY THIRTY MINUTES passed, they were on their fourth round of shots and still no Kari. "Hello, Momma," Ashley muttered.

"What was that?" Emily leaned in close to Ashley. She asked the question even though she knew exactly what the other had said. "The redhead with the tattoos, right?" Emily was surer than ever something had gone wrong between Lauren and her best friend.

Ashley looked at her with a smile. The woman was close to them and had continued to look in their direction throughout her dance. She wore a black skirt and a stomach-revealing tank top. Even from this distance, they could see at least four large tattoos, one particular of a dragon or a reptile as a lot of it was hidden by her tank top disappearing down into her skirt as she moved around on the dance floor with another woman. "You know me too well," Ashley replied. "I would like to trace every bit of her ink with my tongue."

"You are such a guy sometimes," Emily replied with a laugh.

"I can't help it," Ashley replied, attempting to look away from the temptation.

"She may have other things in mind," Emily stated. The other redhead continued to glance back to her friend.

"I'm not the only one to grab the attention of a potential mate," Ashley said. "At the bar, the guy with the short red hair keeps looking over at you. You would make such cute ginger babies together."

Emily stretched forward to get a clear look at the guy. He was skinny and dressed in a long-sleeve, dark-red shirt, and jeans. His hair was dark with shade of red bordering on black from their distance, spiked but neatly cut close.

"You should at least get her number, you know just in case it does not work out between you and Lauren."

Ashley only gave her a look before she moved across the booth and out onto the dance floor. Emily, however, was amused when she skipped past the other woman with only a momentary graze of their arms and a smile. Ashley had other plans as she approached the bar taking a seat next to the man. She could see the two of them talking and watching her. It was not long before Ashley started back, again stopping for a moment to exchange a whisper with the tattooed red-head on the dance floor.

"What did you do?" Emily questioned, as Ashley sat back down at the booth.

"I told him you were single and that I would come back here, stay for a moment and then get up and leave to go dance. And, if he was a creep or anything less than respectful to you, I would cause him more pain than he's ever felt in his adult life."

"He is not going to come over here."

"We will see." Ashley made haste to the dance floor to join the woman she had whispered to moments earlier.

Much to Emily's surprise, the moment Ashley left, the man walked her way.

"Hi, I'm Dexter." The man set a drink down in front of her.

"Sara," she lied, shaking his hand. "Thank you for coming over, but I'm truly not interested," she lied again. She could feel the hunger growing inside her the moment she touched his hand. Dexter just gave her a look before he left her. It was only a few minutes be-fore Ashley returned.

"Come, I'll take you home." Ashley grabbed her by the wrist.

They were at the door when Emily brought them to a stop. "I want you to stay. You've been watching over me all this time. You need to have some fun. I know something went wrong between you and Lauren."

Ashley looked away; there was a pain on her face Emily knew well. Her best friend really liked the nurse.

"Work some of your frustrations away on the cute redhead. I'll have Colin come pick me up." She kissed her friend on the forehead. Emily gave her friend a final glance before exiting. Ashley was watching her with a look of uncertainty.

IT WAS STILL early when she looked at her phone and placed the call. It rang six times before the answering machine picked up. She called again, until finally on the third ring, a voice answered with a resounding angry, "Hello."

"Colin…" There was a long pause, but she could hear him breathing, "…I need you."

Emily sat just inside the entrance of the club, the music still loud on the inside; she watched the flickering street light outside. With each dance, she thought her heart was going to jump from her chest, and the last thing she wanted to do was wait outside. It had been nearly forty minutes from the time she called until she saw headlights coming into the parking lot. She rushed from the building to the locked passenger door, looking around frantically as she waited for him to unlock it. Almost the moment it was opened, she was inside and had the door shut behind her. "Thank you. Thank you," she repeated. She did not hesitate to lock the door.

"What are you doing out here this time of night," he questioned.

"Can we just go," she replied quickly. "Back to your place? I don't want to go home."

Colin gave her a judgmental glare before pulling the vehicle into gear and starting on their way.

———————◆———————

COLIN'S HOME WAS on a secluded hill. There were two ways into the house—a walkway, or two sets of paved steps. Emily rushed up the steps since it was the more direct route to his home. He followed only a couple of steps behind. She was waiting at the door for him to unlock it, and as soon as he did, she rushed inside.

"What is wrong?" Colin questioned.

"I almost made a mistake tonight…with some random guy," she said, watching him lock the door behind them.

The living room was a typical bachelor pad with clothes and stuff strewn everywhere. There was a large black couch, a television on one wall and a fireplace toward the outside. Emily found her way to the couch and stared at the fire. The heat radiated her way as she removed her jacket and placed it on the couch.

"I am glad you called. You should never hesitate when you need something," Colin took off his large flannel jacket revealing a simple white t-shirt and jeans. He pushed his unlaced boots off without even kneeling. "You want a beer?" He walked out of the room and did not even wait for a reply. A moment later, he returned with two opened bottles. He sat one on the small table at the edge of the couch and kept the other in hand.

Emily stared at the door where a couple of packed bags waited. "Are you going somewhere?" she questioned, taking the beer.

"I was supposed to go upstate for a couple of weeks, hunting, being one with the outdoors." Colin leaned back in his chair. "I was supposed to go a couple of weeks back but, well…"

It had been Emily's fault he never went. She'd forgotten he would go away for a couple of weeks—or even as long as a month every year.

"Don't you dare apologize, and even now, I won't hesitate to call it off."

"You should go," Emily replied, sitting back in the comfortable couch. "Actually, I am asking you to go…and don't think twice about it."

"What are you not saying, Emily?" Colin questioned.

She could see the concern in his eyes. Her heart raced—thoughts of tearing into flesh were in her mind more than ever. She tried to fight the thoughts, but there was just too much going on in her mind.

"Do you believe in the supernatural, that there are things in this world that just cannot be explained?" she asked, leaning forward in her seat, the beer in hand.

"You mean like vampires and such?"

"Maybe…I don't know what I mean. Mathew Bradley told me something that I can't get out of mind."

"Not to take away from what he did for you, but Mathew Bradley is an old drunk and you should take everything he said with a pinch of salt."

"All of these deaths and I am the only person to live. The authorities have no idea what it is. Bradley said he saw something that night as he sped away from the scene, after he pulled me into his truck. Something as tall as any man and it howled, Colin." She leaned back, placing the beer on the table. "It fucking howled." She was having a problem fighting back tears as her heart thundered inside her chest.

Colin laughed as he set his own beer down beside hers. "So, we are talking werewolf?"

"I don't know what I'm talking about. The attack, my seizure, the dreams….the damn dreams," she said holding her head in her hands and leaning forward on the couch. "And the other night at dinner…I was feeling perfectly fine, and then I had a hallucination and saw everyone I care for with their throats ripped out."

Colin got up and crossed the room. Sitting down beside her, he pulled her back against him, her legs still pulled up against her body.

"Em, listen to me…you have been through a lot and you are letting the ramblings of an old man drive you…"

"Crazy. I know how I sound…it is how I feel as well," she quickly replied as tears began to flow freely.

Colin wrapped his arm around her pulling her closer against his chest.

"Werewolf…" It was the first time she'd said it out loud even though she had thought about it a lot since she spoke to Bradley. Emily could never bring herself to say it. Saying it made her feel ill, as if she had knowingly lost her sanity. "It does sound crazy."

"You are going through a rough time," he proclaimed. "This will all pass and we will laugh about this conversation one day." There was long pause of silence, only the crackle of fire filled the room. "About the other night…we have been friends since our senior year in high school. And I would be lying if I said I'd never thought about us in that way, but I could not take advantage of you."

She shifted her head looking back at him. "You would not have been taking advantage; I wanted you…very badly."

"And now?" he questioned.

He got his reply in the form of a soft kiss on his lips. She shifted where she could look into his eyes in a more comfortable position. "Only if you are comfortable with this," she stated, not waiting for a reply as she shifted into a cradling position on his lap.

His hand drifted up her legs just under her loose dress. "I think I am," he replied.

Emily felt his soft lips on hers. She pulled away for just a moment as his scruff tickled, and then kissed him again. Their lips parted as they kissed allowing a hint of tongue. His hands rested on her legs just under the dress, while hers fought with the belts around her. The first fell to the floor behind them followed shortly by the second—freeing the dress and allowing her to breathe easier without the binding leather.

Emily pulled at his shirt until he raised his arms allowing it to come free. She tossed it on the floor behind the couch. She kissed him on his neck, softly and repeatedly. Emily felt his body fall lower into the couch, a comfortable position as she kissed his chest. She let her teeth graze skin feeling him flinch. She smiled.

"Hey!"

'Sorry," she muttered with a mischievous grin as their eyes met and their lips again touched. Her hands roamed freely at his jeans, pulling the latch and the zipper free, she was surprised to find nothing else there. He was wearing no underwear under his jeans. She rose as he pushed them down his hips before he sat free and she again cradled him. She could feel his bare legs rub against her own under the dress, his hands still ran just under the dress, but no farther.

"Don't," she whispered, "don't hold back." She felt his hand on the inside of her thigh. Slowly he moved his hand up and down her leg and each touch sent a shiver of excitement up her body. His other hand rested on her clothed hip for only a moment before moving to her breasts. Even through the layers of clothing, she knew he could feel her hard nipple. The very touch caused her to sigh and take a deep breath as his hand rubbed the inside of her legs. She rested her forehead on his. Their eyes met as she ran a hand down between them. She felt him under her dress on the inside of her leg causing her to arch into him. She bit her lip and closed her eyes as she reached back unzipping the top of her dress. She pulled it down her arms exposing her bra. Just as suddenly, Colin buried his face in her cleavage. Emily placed a hand on the back of his head and pulled him closer. His scruff against her breasts and the touch of his lips made her smile.

Emily pulled the band from her hair as she felt him pull the bra down exposing her breasts fully to him. His free hand firmly placed her nipple between his lips and he caressed it with his tongue. The entire time he looked up at her, and she smiled looking into his eyes. She grabbed a handful of hair pulling his head back so he would look up as she kissed him again. She could feel the hand under her dress as it pulled at her panties with little success until she stopped to help. Still sitting with the dress around her hips she cradled him and could feel his erection. She again pushed her hand down between them, taking him in her hand. She smiled when he smiled and watched him bite his lower lip as she slowly moved her hand back-and-forth. She lowered herself down onto his lap; her eyes closed feeling him inside her. She leaned back. She could feel the grip of his strong hand on her back holding her in place, stopping her from falling to the floor. The other hand on her hip as she moved against him and then away repeatedly. Their breathing grew faster and louder. She kept her eyes closed, biting her lower lip. She could feel his grip tighten.

Emily felt his lips on her shoulder. She opened her eyes as his mouth trailed across her collarbone until he reached her neck. She ran her hands through his shaggy hair while his rough tongue traced her neck for a moment before trailing down to her breasts. His tongue on her nipple caused a delighted whimper to escape her. She pushed the sweat-covered hair from her face. Emily pulled his hair, forcing his head back. She let her eyes linger on his for a moment before she kissed his lips—more intensely and passionately than before. She pulled away, biting down on his lower lip a moment before she released it. They both smiled. She felt his hands crossover her legs and he shifted their bodies to the edge of the couch. He stood, keeping her tight against his body, as she pressed her thighs against him, her arms wrapped around his neck to hold steady.

"Don't drop me." She wrinkled her nose.

"Trust me." Colin smiled as they looked at each other, step-by-step he moved toward the fireplace.

"How romantic." Emily giggled.

He let her down reaching for the blanket on the edge of the couch and laid it on the floor in front of the fireplace. "Shush." He smiled, tossing the pillow down with the blanket. He grabbed her by the dress and pulled her closer, mirroring their last kiss. Slowly they lowered to the floor, Emily with her head comfortably engulfed in the pillow. She smiled watching Colin sit above her. She wrapped her legs around his hips pulling him closer. Her hands rested on his hips, while his hands sat like statues on each side of her, holding his position over top of her.

"I now see why all those cheerleaders loved you in high school, daddies little girls they weren't," she muttered.

"You were always too interested in my brother to notice me," Colin quipped.

She wanted to growl, but he was right. "I don't think you want me thinking about your brother right now," she replied.

Emily smiled. She gasped as she felt him inside her again. She moaned, much louder than before, as she moved and grabbed a handful of hair. Biting her lip did nothing as she pulled him down on top of her body. "Oh my," she whined out, arching up against him.

She clasped a hand over her mouth in an attempt to muffle the sounds escaping her. She could tell she was blushing. Her free hand pulled Colin's head closer to her own as she kissed him, but he did not slow his movements. Her entire body arched in pleasure and ecstasy.

Emily held him close as she turned, rolling onto her stomach. She rested comfortably on her hands and knees, her eyes staring into the fire. She felt his strong hands on her hips, positioning himself behind her. She dropped her head into the pillow when he pushed himself inside. She wanted to scream out. She bit on the pillow, his motion getting faster and faster, the contact of their bodies was deafening. She gripped the pillow tightly, feeling one of his hands leave her body. She felt the tug on her hair bringing her back up in the air. A tight grip, he was going so fast now she only wanted to scream harder but nothing came out as she gritted her teeth trying to quiet herself. She felt herself tighten around him. And then he pulled harder until she was kneeling with her back against his body, still arched against him, he did not slow as he twisted, kissing her lips.

As their lips touched, Emily felt it deep down, something different from the rest of the feelings and emotions running rampant in her body. She had only felt this once before…the night of her seizure. A deep growing pain in her stomach, she felt herself spasm, her body was revolting. She was orgasming, but more. It was happening again. With strength, she never knew she possessed, she pushed against Colin, but he was no longer there. She heard him mumble, "What the hell?"

The change was coming and she wanted it to stop, she needed it to stop. She rolled over into a fetal position, every muscle and bone in her body seemed to move. "Oh Christ," she heard him say just before the touch of his hand on her shoulder.

"Don't fucking touch me," she called out in a hoarse voice bordering on a growl. She swiped a hand across his chest. Colin fell to the floor and immediately grabbed at the long, deep scratches as they began to bleed. She could see him, through the tears and the haze, as he looked around frantically. He placed his shirt against the wounds before returning to her side.

"I'm calling an ambulance."

He was gone from her sight now, "Don't," she called out in the same harsh voice. Rolling over onto her hands and knees, she began to crawl.

"Emily…"

She did not have to see his face; she could hear the horror in his voice. She could feel every muscle in her body move under her skin and she knew he could see it. Her red mane, matted with sweat, stuck to her face. Her eyes changed. Gone was her natural color, changed to an intense yellow and red.

"Help me," she whispered, almost back to her natural soft voice. He immediately rushed to her side just as she screamed out in pain again. He rolled her into a seated position and started to hold her in his arms.

"What is happening to you?" he questioned, fighting back the tears as she repeatedly screamed out in pain.

Every movement hurt more than the last. "Help me," she muttered as sweat and tears poured from her. She could see the horror in Colin's eyes. His hands trembled as she held them tightly. Her nails grew and they both could see it and she felt his arm release its grip around her body. She pulled away again, feeling the spasms growing more violent. She felt her gums split, she could taste blood in the back of her throat, and she knew her teeth were razor sharp. Her tongue pressed against them. Colin leaned down over top of her, his eyes were bloodshot and she tried to smile. She wanted to say the word again, *werewolf,* but she had no voice. Only a growl. She saw him hesitate.

Again, she tried to speak but this time it came as a scream and he moved toward her again. He looked around; she knew what he was searching for. A phone. He wanted to call for help. "Don't." She forced the word shaking her head. He leaned in and she pushed again he was gone from site and she blacked out.

------------◆------------

EMILY WOKE. SHE felt the cool touch of covers against her naked body. She rose in the bed pulling them tight against her. A glance to the window confirmed it was still dark outside. The stench of a cheap cigar filled the dark room. She sat with her head in her hands.

"How do you feel?" Colin's voice broke the silence.

"It was all real, wasn't it?" Emily questioned.

"Every nightmarish, blood-chilling scream, every grotesque, unnatural flesh-crawling moment." He took another draw from his cigar.

"Wish I could wake from this nightmare." She pushed the hair from her face.

"I wish you could too, but now we have a problem and I don't know what to do, Em. I don't even know where to turn to get you help…without getting me locked up in a loony bin. Or worse, they believe me…what then?" Colin questioned, reaching to turn on a shaded lamp near him.

"They lock me up and experiment on me."

"We won't let either happen, there has to be something we can do…someone we can go to…" he said with uncertainty.

"I feel him…I know I did not kill Troy but I have the ache, the dream I had was more than just a dream. I am connected to the other one…"

"He is a murderer…he has embraced what he is…we do not need to seek him out until we know more." Colin watched as Emily lay back in the bed.

"The excitement of the night…I think it caused the spasm, the animal within waking maybe? Gives a whole new meaning to the phrase an 'animal in bed'."

He smiled.

Emily rested her hand on her forehead. "What do we do now?"

"You listen to your body. You need to avoid highly emotional situations…we don't know if it is a true trigger to your attacks. And after what I saw last night…how far it will go?" he wondered.

"I feel it Colin…It is not a matter of how far will it go. It is when will I go? When will I turn into that thing from my nightmares? The last night in the hospital…the night before we made out. You, like so many others in my life, were in the dream but the last thing I saw in my head was me. A naked, blood-soaked feral version of myself…'

"I think I met her last night." He lifted his shirt to show the bandage on his chest. "I would ask you to cut your nails but with everything I witnessed it won't matter."

"We need a plan…for when it happens…"

"I have already thought of that, both seizure attacks happened at night…it is obvious the moon cycle means shit to the transformation as the Alpha has killed at all settings of the moon. But maybe the moon does have something to do with it, the darkness that comes with it."

"Lock me away during the night?" Emily questioned.

"Not just yet…I think you will know, now that we are more aware of what is happening and we know you aren't just crazy," he said with a half-smile. "There is something we are missing."

"The other…he would know," Emily replied.

"We will not go looking for him. I think you living was an accident, he fully intended on killing you. As far as we know, he could be stalking you even now to hide the realism of what is happening. Or worse…now that you are 'infected' he may consider you a potential mate."

It was something she had not thought of until that moment.

"There is a man…I saw him yesterday watching me…I felt his eyes on me, I knew him, Colin, I felt him under my skin. It was him…"

Colin sat back in his chair putting his cigar out in the ashtray. "Get some sleep, Em, you need your rest. There is a lot we don't know and we need to separate fact from fiction first. We will talk more in the morning." Colin got up, leaving the room. Emily pulled the covers close, shutting her eyes knowing she would not sleep. Now she knew what she was. She was a werewolf.

13

EMILY WOKE SUDDENLY. Her heart raced as she arched her back lifting her chest into the air, twisting her head and neck in an awkward position. She wheezed heavily but no air came to her. Hands ripped and tugged at the bed covers as her naked body thirsted for oxygen. She repeatedly gasped until her body fell back to the covers. She twisted and fell to the floor with a loud crash knocking into the end table. It remained standing but all of its contents fell to the floor. She twisted to her back, and for the first time since she woke, she could breathe. She took several deep breaths before she sat up straight.

"Colin," she choked, turning to look at the door and then at the window where sunshine beat through the glass. "Colin."

She pulled the sheet from the bed wrapping it around her as she walked from the bedroom to the living room, but still no Colin in sight. She did not stop moving until she found herself sitting on the couch. She tossed the sheet from her naked body and quickly began to gather her clothing. Her green lace bra and panties were on top of her freshly washed green dress. She smiled as she dressed. She put both of her belts on and brought her tall knee-high boots over to the couch where she put them on. She had just stood when the door crept open.

"You're awake." Colin placed a cup holder on the counter. "Butterscotch cappuccino, nothing like a hot coffee on a cold morning." Colin raised his into the air crossing the room and sat in the chair across from her. "Are you going somewhere?"

"Home."

"And then what?"

"I don't know."

"Go about your day-to-day until you fully turn and kill someone—your parents or Ashley?" Colin questioned.

She looked at him with anger. "Then I should stay here?" she questioned sitting back down, her knees together and feet twisted out. "This won't work…you want me to keep my emotions in check? You can't lock me up, not around you. The other night I was like a dog in heat, no pun intended. I wanted you so bad. Same thing with Troy. I have always loved you as a friend…but my human side isn't in control of my hormones, Colin."

"We need a sensible plan," Colin replied. He had a cocky smile as he looked down at the floor between them.

"Sensible? I would settle for batshit crazy at this point," Emily said with a half-smile.

"You can go home, but maybe you need to convince Ashley you are alright…and maybe she should not stay over anymore," Colin stated as their eyes met. "I know that won't be easy."

"I can handle Ashley." Emily returned the smile.

"She may like that," Colin replied.

"Don't be a pervert," she stated, standing and walking across the room to her own cappuccino. "Now, will you take me home?"

"Yes, my lady," Colin replied.

———————●———————

THE DRIVE WAS silent, neither wanted to face the subject at hand. They pulled into her driveway and Emily exhaled an obvious sigh of relief. Ashley was not there. She exited the truck walking to her door. There was a hand-written note:

Call Me!!!
~ Ashley

"You sure you can convince her to leave you home alone?" Colin questioned.

"She let me go home with a guy, I'm sure I can convince her I can handle myself alone," Emily said as she unlocked the door. "Also…can we keep last night between us?"

"The whole she-wolf thing or the sex?" Colin questioned with a mischievous grin, attempting to make her smile.

"Both…" Emily stepped inside.

"So you would rather let your best friend think you spent the night with a total stranger than me? I am hurt," Colin said as he followed her inside.

"How are you handling this so well?"

Colin looked away then back at her. "In the past when I've told you I'd be there for you I meant it. For any reason, I'm here for you. I thought I had lost you in the attack…but you survived. Now this…I know you will find a way to get through this. And I'll be at your side."

Emily gave him a half-smile. "You've always been a great friend. Which is why I hate to ask you this, but I think I need some time to myself Colin. I need to process and I can't do that with you playing shadow," Emily replied, turning at the end of the counter to look at her friend.

"Call me tonight, and we should have lunch tomorrow…we will figure this out." He approached her, kissing her on the forehead. "Trust me." He turned, leaving the house and shutting the door behind him.

"I trust you, Colin, but I think I have to do this alone," she stated, approaching the door and watching until he was gone before grabbing her keys and rushing off to her garage.

EMILY PULLED HER jeep into the short driveway leading up to her parent's one-story brick home. During the three-hour drive, she had not considered what she was going to say…until this moment. She turned the engine off and sat with her head against the steering wheel. Taking a deep breath, she opened the door. It had been a while since she'd visited her parents' home. Again, she hesitated at the door as she looked back at her vehicle, and then turned and knocked on the door. It opened almost immediately.

"You know better than to knock."

Her mom was there waiting, she must have heard her as she pulled into the driveway. "Your father is gone but I expect him back shortly."

Emily smiled, walking past her and into her childhood home. She took a moment just inside the door, it always marveled her how little the house had changed since she was a little kid. The only real change was the updated red living room set, and new pictures added to the walls some as old as when she was a baby.

"Ashley called for you earlier, she sounded worried but then assured me you were with Colin and she was just tired of waiting."

Emily smiled. Ashley was covering for her, again.

"Yeah, I met Colin…for breakfast," Emily said glancing at the old wooden wall clock and checking the time. It was still hours before dark.

"Does this mean you won't be staying for dinner?" her mom questioned.

"Sorry, I just wanted to stop by and get something from my old room," Emily replied, "—if that is all right?" Even though little remained in her childhood room, it was a valid excuse.

"Honey, you never need to ask," her mom replied with a large smile.

Emily returned the smile before she disappeared down the hall.

<hr>

EMILY WALKED TO the end of the hall turning back to look, her mother was nowhere to be seen. She quickly stepped into a room, but not hers. She crossed the room to the old willow tree figure and pulled a key from a branch. Quickly dropping to her knees and peeking under her parents' bed, she pulled out a small white case. She dragged it free and unlocked it. She paused as she glared at the contents. She hated guns. The small .357 snub nose stared back at her—the black metal glistened in the light. The rough black handle seemed to call to her and she picked it up from the velvet cloth it was nestled in. Her hands were petite but the gun still fit in her palm. She was surprised at the weight. She set it on the floor and picked up the small box of shells that were hidden under the cloth before she shut the box and pushed it back under the bed.

Emily stepped out into the hall glancing toward the end, no one to be seen. She quickly ducked into her old room weapon and box of shells in hand. She set them on the old dresser and opened the top drawer—pulling out an old purse. Torn and worn with age, little ducklings littered the design. It was a gift from her grandmother, she was not very sentimental, but the thought of her nanny caused her to take a deep breath. She quickly unzipped it placing the gun and box inside. She paused again after she shut the drawer and looked around the room at all the stuff from her childhood. Emily exhaled her breath not realizing she had still been holding it before she exited the room with purse in hand.

She entered the living room looking toward the kitchen, her mom's back was to her as she walked to the door and set the purse down among shoes.

"Did you find what you were looking for?" her mom called out.

Emily is startled when her mom asks if she found what she was looking for. She's quickly and nervously looking into the kitchen again to be sure her mom's back is still turned.

"Yes," she paused looking at the purse on the floor. "Mom, do you mind if I wear your sandals?"

"Course not, dear," she replied.

Emily quickly unzipped her boots pulling them free and put the small purse inside of one. She slipped the sandals on before she walked to the kitchen. Her mom turned and smiled as her daughter entered the room, her hair had seemed to gray twice as much as the last time she had seen her. Gone were her auburn locks, replaced by dyed brown and gray.

"I am glad you stopped by, you are looking better now."

Emily was glad she thought so but knew the truth.

"And I love your dress."

Emily glanced down at the green dress she had been wearing on-and-off for nearly twenty-four hours. "Thank you," she replied.

"So why did you really stop by? I know it was not for some ratty old purse," she turned, drying her hands, a large smile across her face.

Emily gasped wondering just how much her mother had seen.

"You drove three hours to get it, something's wrong."

"I need to go…" she said. "I just wanted to stop by and say I was sorry for all the worrying I have caused as of late and I love you both."

"Dear, we know you love us, and we love you," her mom replied.

Emily crossed the room and gave her mom a big hug, for a moment she did not to want to let go.

"Your heart is racing, dear—are you sure you are all right?"

"I am fine, Mom. Just have a lot on my mind. You know," she replied. "But I do have to go."

"You should wait for your father," she replied.

"Just tell him what I said. I want to get home before dark…and before Ashley calls out the National Guard." Emily turned, leaving the room. Her mom watched her every step as she grabbed her boots at the door and left her parents' home.

Emily stopped at the edge of the porch and looked down at the small suburban neighborhood. It had changed so much in just a few short years.

"You know, I'm making your favorite food…"

Emily turned. Her mom stood in the doorway wiping her hands clean.

"I know." Emily smiled. She could smell the baked chicken parmesan—had smelled it the moment she exited her car—but didn't want to say anything. If she did, it would make it harder to leave.

"Please, stay."

Emily turned away from her mom. She gritted her teeth. She was starving. "Okay." Emily turned giving her a glance. "Give me a moment." She practically hopped down the stairs and down the path to her car, placing the boots in the back seat. This was a mistake—she took a long deep breath and closed the door—but it would give her a chance to say a proper goodbye to her father. She hugged herself tightly and walked back to the house. She knew this could be the last time she'd see her parents for a while.

"Dinner will be done in a little bit," her mother stated.

Emily never walked back into the kitchen but found herself back in her room. She flopped back on the bed looking up at the off-white textured ceiling. The walls were a light purple, years past needing a fresh coat of paint. She twisted to open the nightstand, which was empty with the exception of a thin photo album. Several photos fell out onto the bed, she scattered them out to look at them. All of them were from her final track meet her senior year—she, her mom, and Ashley were in one...a rival at their high school, Dawn,—she never knew what happened to her after their senior year—in another... and one of Colin with his brother in the background. The last photo was of her and her coach. It was evident how absent her father was from all of the pictures. And while some might assume he'd been the one taking them, Emily knew better. Her father had never come to any of her meets, always having an excuse to be elsewhere.

Emily heard the familiar screech of the front door open. She sat on the edge of her bed; knowing this was a mistake. After last night with Colin, spending a night with her parents—especially her dad—was a big mistake. She walked out into the hall. The moment she did she heard her father's stern voice. She hadn't even realized he was home.

"Where is she?" he questioned in a cold tone. She was flashing back to high school now, the same voice he used when he was disappointed in her for one reason or another.

"In her room," her mother replied with hesitation.

There was pause. Emily stepped back into her room, holding the door ready to shut it. She was having a flashback now. This was nothing new to her. How many times had she stood in her door waiting to see if he was going to come see her? complain about her grades? or how she'd performed in the latest track meet? or to complain about her friends? or music? Any number of reasons...whereas most parents would have been happy with her.

"Leave her alone. I think she just needs a moment to herself."

She heard her father stop his progress down the hall. She was sure she heard him sigh. And though he gave no verbal answer, she knew he was no longer coming to see her.

Emily stepped behind the door shutting it, taking a long deep breath and slow exhale in the process. This was a terrible mistake. Her stomach churned with anxiety. She couldn't find a single memory where she was happy with her father—where he allowed her to just be herself. There was always the projection of who he thought she should be.

She wondered if maybe all parents were like that. Her mom encouraged her to try out for track, and lacrosse too—though admittedly, Lacrosse had been a one-semester and done thing for her once she realized how violent it could be. Her father, however, had scoffed when he learned she was going to go out for the sport. She could still remember his disappointing glare when she'd said she wasn't going to take up a second season.

Emily needed to leave. She crossed to the back of the room opening the window—the same window she had slipped in and out of a number of times her junior year when she and Colin's brother, Derrick, were a thing. She was sure her parents never knew. She pushed the curtains to one side.

"Hey."

It felt like she stopped breathing. Maybe if she didn't reply he'd leave and she could finish her escape.

"I'm glad you came by."

She inhaled, standing up straight and turning to face her father. Emily turned, her father stood in the door. He had removed his tie and jacket.

"I wanted to see you and Mom," she replied.

"You're lying," he said so bluntly it sent a chill up Emily's back.

She had come for the gun. Colin never gave her his and now more than ever she needed one. For a moment, she thought he knew, but it only took a moment for her to convince herself he didn't. He was just being her dad. She could have left but was sure if she had, they'd been having this conversation over the phone. Either way, there was no escaping him.

"No…I know this has been rough on you since my accident, and you've worried about me," she lied. She was not convincing him either, she could tell by the twitch of his lip into a half-smile.

"I'm here," he turned in the doorway, "if you want to talk about it."

"I know," Emily replied. She breathed a sigh of relief once he disappeared from sight.

She flopped back on the bed. She twisted gathering the photos and album, quickly returning them back to their hiding spot. She looked at her cell phone, a couple texts from Ashley. She tucked it into her back pocket as she exited the room. She gave a knock on her father's office door before opening it. She was never allowed in this room when she was growing up. It was his space and she rarely even remembered her mother being in there. The room was twice the size of her bedroom, and there was only one other room in the house bigger. She was surprised she didn't find him there. It used to be his routine to lock himself in his study for hours after getting home from work. She glanced around the room. The walls were littered with awards and newspaper articles—almost all of which were about him. There were some pertaining to their extended family, but Emily could see only one reference to her—an article about her coming in 2nd at a local track meet. Of all the races she'd won, that was the article he'd clipped and hung. No pictures of her. She often wondered if she was such a disappointment, why they didn't have more children. She could never remember the topic even being discussed between them, and she had never asked.

Emily spanned the room, taking it all in—the articles praising his therapy practice, a picture of him and Dr. Knox—she was sure her mother loved that. She crossed over to behind the desk, it was clear, but then she saw the family picture. It was her freshman year in high school, the three of them standing in front of a large flower bush with white blossoms. All she could think when she saw it was how pale she looked…as transparent as the blossoms in the background. Her dark-red hair looked orange in the sunlight. She couldn't help but think how hideous she appeared.

The door creeping open broke her gaze. Emily could see the disappointment on his face, she'd been caught in the one place he never wanted her.

"Your mom wanted me to tell you, dinner is done." He forced a smile.

She wondered if his patients got that fake smile as often as she did. He never complained, just turned, and left his office. She took a moment to look around before following suit. She was starving.

***

THEY HAD BEEN into their dinner less than ten minutes when Emily put her fork down, a parent on each side of her. She looked forward after glancing at both. "I'm a werewolf." She imagined saying it, taking a deep breath, holding it waiting for their reaction. She figured her mom wouldn't say anything. Her dad, however, would likely have her committed within an hour of actually saying it. She wondered how that would go over, locked in a hospital ward with lots of people with issues of their own. How long before the wolf came out…

The sound of her father talking broke her from her daydream. "Huh?" She hadn't heard a word he said.

"When are you going back to work?" He might as well have said *why are you here.*

"I'm not sure," Emily retorted. "I'm on medical leave for another week," she lied. She hadn't been in touch with the firm she worked for, but she knew they were aware of what had happened to her—at least as much as anyone else. But, she had not called in since she had gotten out of the hospital the first time. She was unsure which would make her father more disappointed: the fact that she hadn't been in touch with her job? or the fact that she had been content at a job he would have considered no more than a glorified secretary? She could hear him chew his food loudly causing her to sigh.

"I have friends who are looking for business aids," her father said coldly. He wasn't looking at her; his eyes remained on her mother across the table.

"I like my job," Emily growled. It wasn't a lie. She did like her job at the law firm. She didn't work crazy hours. Her boss, Mr. Walters, often let them leave early on Fridays if he didn't have a hefty caseload with pay. His partner and wife ought dinner for the office a couple times a week. She knew now, she needed to call them tomorrow.

"Yeah," her father replied with a grumble of his own.

"No but, I have a good job. I support myself," Emily snarled. She didn't realize her lip was twitching until after she spoke. "I don't ask anything of you, now do I?"

"Your dad didn't—"

"The hell he didn't," Emily felt her temperature rise. Her stomach churned. There was more than just frustration and anger growing in her. It was only made worse by her mother's defense of him. She slapped her napkin on the table and pushed her chair under it in one fluid motion. "I'm going for a walk." She had to. She needed to calm down.

<hr>

EMILY FELT LUCKY. She didn't want to wear the same clothes on her walk, fortunately she discovered a duffel full of workout clothes in the back of her jeep that hadn't been worn, yoga pants and a short sleeve black t-shirt, as well as her running shoes. She was a mile away from her parents' house when she reached the old running trail used by the nearby schools for their track and field programs.

The trail led up several steep embankments that Emily found quite easy to climb. She picked up the pace with every obstacle. It had been years since she ran this trail but it did not seem to change. She topped the hill leading to an old strip-mining project. The moon hung high overhead, she leaned over catching her breath and looking up at the half oval. It was only a half moon, but the sky was so clear it still looked full. She wondered how the cycle of the moon would have an effect on her. The air was cold, she had heard the rumors about possible snow in the forecast. It wasn't something she had noticed until now, she usually froze so easily.

Emily started to walk the trail, watching the moon as she reached the tallest peak around. She took a long deep breath and let out a yell as if she was howling at the moon. She laughed when she ran out of oxygen and could no longer sustain the noise.

IT WAS NEARLY 2:00 a.m. when Emily found herself approaching her parents' driveway again. She walked to her jeep, slipped the key from her pocket and unlocked the door.

"Are you just going to leave without saying goodbye?"

His voice should have startled her, but she had expected he would be there waiting.

"Or, 'I love you' to your mother?"

"I love you too, Father," Emily sighed. "I wasn't going to just leave." She never called him that, it was always Dad or Daddy.

"I don't know if I believe you."

Emily let her forehead fall to her jeep. "Of course you don't. You always think so little of me, no matter what I do." She looked up seeing the door close. It took all of a minute for her father to piss her off again and cause the tension in her stomach to return. She grabbed a notebook from the backseat quickly scribbling a note:

I love you. And I am sorry.
Emily

Emily pushed the note under the door before getting into her jeep and driving off. She knew she couldn't face him. Trying to explain to him what was wrong would only make her angry. And she did not know what would happen then.

———◆———

EMILY SET HER boots beside the entrance of her home pulling the purse free and set it on the counter. She closed and locked the door behind her, going so far as to latch the deadbolt. She glanced outside. She'd left her car in the driveway…an odd thing for her to do. Maybe she should have parked it back in the garage. She placed her head against the door and took a deep breath before walking into the kitchen.

Brushing a wayward curl from her forehead with one hand, Emily tugged at the Frigidaire's door with the other and tried to remember if there was any cherry brandy left. Jostled by the swinging of the heavy 'fridge door, the sleek glass bottle rolled from behind a carton of expired milk and last night's Chinese takeout. With an appreciative sigh, Emily freed the bottle from its icy metal prison.

Searching for a clean cognac glass proved to be a bit more difficult than locating the liquor, so Emily settled for a coffee cup. Her right hand juggled the bottle and mug, leaving her left hand free to dig through the freezer for a couple of blocks of ice, which Emily promptly deposited into the world's ugliest cup. An old birthday gift from Troy. Pouring the whiskey with careful precision as she lowered her tired body onto a second-hand barstool, Emily decided there was nothing wrong with drinking brandy from a goblet with a dancing pig on it.

Emily stared at her drink through tear-filled eyes. The chime of a wall clock broke her from her daze. 6:00 a.m., it would be daylight soon. She got up from her stool, leaving the room only to return a moment later with pen and paper in hand. She sat back at the counter, and finished off her drink in one swallow. The ice was mostly melted now but it did not stop her from refilling it to dissolve what was left. She looked at the blank page taking a deep breath and started to write.

Ash –

I sit here writing this with great pain inside me. Stuff I would like to tell you but I could not. You are the last person I would want to give me the confused look, to think I was crazy. For a time I thought I was for reasons I cannot explain in writing. Part of me still does not believe it. I don't want to believe, I would like to wake up and everything be alright and normal.

It hurts so much, I cannot describe and I know no other way to deal with this. I don't want to become a...monster. Pills arent enough to stop what is inside me. The growing anger, lust, hatred...hollowness within and if I don't stop it now I fear I may hurt someone else. Or kill them. And in all likeliness it would be the one person I care about more so than maybe anyone else. I love you sister. We may not have been blood but to me you were more than just a friend.

I have accepted what I must do. I have said my goodbyes to everyone else. I fear if I were to see you face to face you would know instantly something was wrong. I can't risk it, I'm sorry.

Em

Emily placed the folded letter on the counter, followed by her cell phone. She took a deep breath, and finished another shot of brandy. The tears had stopped flowing, but they had left her eyes puffy. She glared at the .357. She could almost see her reflection in the shine of the metal. She put her hand over the weapon in an attempt to not look at her mirror image. She lowered her forehead to the counter as she took another deep breath. "It's the only way," she muttered out loud with a deep breath. She still felt the anger from her visit with her parents.

Emily sat up with a breath of confidence, taking the weapon in her hands, she opened the revolver, and one-by-one loaded the bullets until it would hold no more. She placed her hands on the counter, her grip on the weapon so tight her knuckles had started to turn white. "What's worse Emily? Becoming a monster and killing someone you love, or stopping the thing before it can even start?" She smiled, quickly picked the gun up and placed the tip of the barrel to her chest. Several quick breaths, she pulled the hammer back and then screamed as she pulled the trigger. She had moved her hand forward just as she pulled the trigger. She placed the gun on the counter in front of her. Her heart raced and the tears began again.

Emily grabbed the cherry brandy, unscrewed the top, took two gulps and screamed as loud as she could before dissolving into unexpected laughter. "I'm not going to give in to you..." She looked at the weapon almost as if she could again see her reflection laughing at her. It all came to her, as everything flashed before her eyes. "If that bastard has some control over what he does while he is the beast...then so will I." She put the gun back into its case and carefully placed it into the old purse before rushing it off to the bedroom. She would have to worry about sneaking it back into her parents' home later. Right now...she had a bullet hole she needed to hide.

———————◆———————

TEN MINUTES HAD passed when Emily found her way to the couch wearing a black tank top and flowered shorts, she pulled the blanket over her toes and nested the bottle of brandy at her side on the couch. She held a tight grip on the glass. Her head rested comfortably on the couch. The tears had once again stopped, but she had made no effort to clean her face. Four thunderous knocks startled her, sending a splitting chill down her back. They were soon followed by four more. It was no coincidence. The gunshot had been heard.

Emily set the bottle of brandy on the table and walked across the room. She opened the door without hesitation or any attempt to see who was on the other side. She did not expect to see the two people who were waiting.

"Detectives, come on in." Emily walked away from the door and found her way back to the couch, and brought the blanket back over her toes. She took the bottle in hand and held it in the air. "Can I offer the two of you a drink?" She smiled. Her head crashed into the arm of the couch with a hollow thud. She had not slept since the night at Colin's. She rubbed at the spot she hit.

"We heard reports of a gunshot, Ms. Meyer." Rebecca Vance was the first of the two into the home. The two of them were dressed very similar, in their black suits over a white shirt, down to their polished black boots.

"I heard it too. It is hunting season, I believe." Emily took a drink watching the detective. The look the woman gave her made her angrier by the second, almost as fierce as the feeling from the dinner with her parents. "So which one are you? I'm thinking Scully? And that would make you Mulder," Emily stated making a reference to two fictional F.B.I. agents from a television series.

"Did you fire off a gun, Ms. Meyer?" Vance was now at the end of the counter looking all around, hand on her hip not far from her gun. "Are you armed, Ms. Meyer?"

Emily leaned forward placing the bottle on the table, standing with a slight stumble. She was tipsy and on the edge of being hysterical. "You can search me if you want," she said, turning in slow motion with her arms held high in the air. "But I would prefer if he did it. Looks like you have strong hands."

"Please don't make any sudden movements, Ms. Meyer," Vance stated walking past the back of the couch and looking around the bathroom before turning back into the living room.

"Ms. Meyer is my mother," Emily said slowly, twisting her body to look back at the female detective and then at Hastings—who sat in front of her leaning on a stool. He smiled as their eyes met... "Tell me, Detective, is she always such a bitch?"

"I would appreciate some respect," Vance called out. She was now only a couple of steps away from Emily and easily within arms reach. "Now, could you answer my questions?"

Emily started to turn, but before she could, Vance had pulled her left arm around behind her. The movement pulled the tank top up to expose her stomach and Hastings paused looking at the healing bite on her left side.

"I heard the gunshot, I promise you it was not me," Emily lied, her heart beating faster. Her expression went blank as she lowered her head until her chin touched her chest and her red hair partially hid her half-smile from Hastings.

"Stand still, I will release your arm if you hold the other one out to the side." Emily nodded, holding both arms out as straight as she could in her drunken state.

Vance began to run her hands up her sides and into her hair.

"I could be wrong. You have quite strong hands as well. My friend would probably like you more than I would though." A slight giggle escaped her as once again looked at Hastings.

"That's enough, Vance." Hastings smiled. "Obviously she is not packing. It would be hard to hide a gun of any sort in those shorts or that top."

"Thank you for noticing," Emily replied. She did not have to see the other woman to know she had backed off, or that she was breathing much heavier, pissed over being told to quit harassing her. "I do work out—try to keep my girlish figure—when I'm not getting mauled by wild, murderous beasts, that is." She took a seat on the couch and eyed, Hastings, feeling a familiar hunger in her stomach.

Hastings walked across the room picking up the bottle from the table. "Harsh stuff, Emily. Tastes like cherry soda dipped in acid, if I remember correctly." He brought it to his lips taking a small drink before he set it back down with a cough.

"We were in the area," Vance said.

"I am sure you were." Emily glanced back at Vance and smiled.

"We understand you have been through a lot, Ms. Meyer." Vance circled around in front of her, but she gave an angry glance toward Hastings.

"Like being attacked by a rabid, supernatural beast? Or being accused of murdering my former lover? At the moment, I'm not sure which is worse." She glared at the other woman, showing her teeth the way a wolf or dog would to warn another predator off.

Vance gave Hastings another glare before leaving the house, but he did not move. "I am sorry about her."

"She needs a good fuck," Emily said with a big grin. "A good fuck can be a cure-all."

"We just wanted to check in and make sure you were alright." Hastings stepped forward and took another drink from the bottle, finishing with a similar cough as before. "Just as horrible as I remember." He started for the door and paused, twisting to look back at Emily. "No matter what you think, things will get better, Emily. Nothing is as bad as it seems in hindsight. If you need anything—just someone to talk to—you have my card."

"I will keep that in mind." She leaned forward taking the bottle.

"Take care," Hastings said, turning and leaving the house with a smile.

Emily did not move from the couch until she was sure they were gone. She took another drink, locked the door, and headed for a cold shower. She knew now, more than ever, she had no control over the feelings she was having.

THE COLD SHOWER did nothing to ease the feelings of lust and anger growing within. Again in the black tank top and floral-pattern shorts, she cleaned the mirror with her wrinkled fingers until she could clearly see her own reflection. "Colin was right. I need to keep my emotions in check." She smiled looking at her still-wet locks as they fell over her face. Her freckles seemed to be more evident when she was cold and her complexion was paler than she could ever remember.

"*Colin was no fun,*" a voice echoed in her head. She looked at her reflection realizing it was her own voice talking back to her.

"What the fuck?" She took a step back from the counter. Even though her face wore an expression of shock and disbelief, the mirror image did not reflect it.

She only smiled and twisted her head to one side.

"This is a dream…"

"*No dream.*"

"A hallucination?" Emily questioned, taking a step forward and watching as the mirror image seemed to take a step back. It took a few more steps until the body of the other Emily could be seen. She lifted her shirt to expose the bite wound, but unlike her own wound, the other Emily's was not healed.

"Your gift. He gave you something precious so few have ever been given, and you almost threw it all away. I am almost sick thinking I'm you." She laughed.

Emily reached for the pill bottle on the counter and quickly opened it. Even though it had been days since she had last taken the medication, she was nearly out.

"Ah, drugs will not help you my dear. What is happening to you cannot be stopped." She continued to trace the bite with her fingers. *Her fingernails dug through the stitches, and blood began to ooze from the old wound.*

Emily felt every cut as she looked down at her own wound, she could almost feel each tear of her own flesh as it happened in the reflection.

"You are running out of time, it will not be long before he comes for you…and you have to let me out."

Emily pulled a rag from the counter top placing it against her wound. She looked at the mirror and her reflection was again normal, a look at the wound and it was normal as well. She paused for a moment to stare intently at her own reflection, before she left the room. She walked through the bedroom and out into the living area. The bottle of cherry brandy—still sitting on the tabletop—had only a few tastes left. She was done with alcohol for the night. The shower had gone a long way to sober her up, and the hallucination finished it. Emily knew it was the lack of sleep. She quickly crawled into bed falling fast asleep.

———————◆———————

EMILY ROLLED OVER looking at the clock, it was after 8 p.m. and she had slept all day. She twisted to look up at the ceiling. With a yawn, she kicked the covers off and crawled out of the bed. Pushing the hair from her face as she crossed into the living room, she picked up the bottle of cherry brandy from the coffee table. She had just twisted the top back on when the knock came. It was loud, consistent, and obnoxious in its repetitive thunder. She set the bottle on the counter, cautiously approaching the door.

Emily was surprised to see Kari on the other side of the peephole. As she opened the door, the petite woman did not hesitate, barging inside. She gave her a quick, polite hug after her rude entrance. "Ashley sends her regards, and she has to pull a double. So she sent entertainment." Kari stood in the doorway and waved. Emily peeked to see several people getting out of the vehicle heading toward her home.

Kari looked like she was dressed much the same way as she had been at the club: plaid schoolgirl skirt, red fishnet stockings, and red boots that looked like they weighed as much as she did. Her black tank top, similar to the one Emily wore, was paired with fingerless gloves that extended all the way to her elbow—a solid one on the hand to hide her scar, while the other was red fishnet.

"I'm really not in the partying mood," Emily proclaimed, turning to see at least four people approaching the house. She sighed.

"We're here on orders from Ash," Kari announced with a spunky smile. It was almost intoxicating how happy she seemed most days.

Emily stepped away from the door just as the first person entered. A young Asian man, possibly several years younger than Emily, smiled slyly. He wore a plain black, long-sleeve shirt with jeans and tennis shoes.

"Jake, I know him from work," Kari said.

The second intruder—a woman dressed a lot like Emily had seen Ashley dress in the past—wore black cargo pants with chains hanging from each pocket, and a netted, black tank top over a white t-shirt. Her main accessory was on her fingers, she wore more rings than Emily could count. The woman also wore black lipstick and purple eyeliner, and she had shoulder-length black hair. The woman held up a couple of bottles of alcohol. Emily did not look at them as she placed them on the counter beside the bottle of brandy.

"Melissa, another coworker," Kari said.

The third interloper had dark skin and a frizzy Afro, but the first thing Emily noticed about her was her large, expressive smile—it was hard to miss. It was also hard not to smile back at her. Her energy was intoxicating.

"I'm Christina, but please call me Ris, or Chris." Her hair tickled Emily's face as she stepped up and gave her an overly-friendly hug. She held her for a moment longer than comfortable. and Emily tried to pull away. She finally released her with an even larger smile. She wore a black, asymmetric-hem dancer's dress over denim jeans. The woman looked fit and was petite in a healthy way.

"And last, but not least, this is, Devon."

The man standing in the doorway wore a long-sleeve shirt with jeans and boots. He was freshly-shaven, with short, dark hair, very clean cut. A black rope necklace hung at his throat, and Emily immediately noticed the wolf emblem at the end. She stared at it for a moment then looked into his dark brown eyes. He smiled. Late twenties, early thirties, and everything about him sent a chill down Emily's back when their eyes met.

Kari kissed the man, hugging him tightly in the process. "I met him the other night when we were out—is he not just a doll?"

"You must be Emily. I've heard so much about you." Devon stepped away from Kari, took Emily's hand, and bowed as he kissed her knuckles.

Emily looked from Devon to Kari with a questioning glare.

"I do hope we are not intruding," He walked around her, farther into her home.

"Isn't he a sweetheart…" Emily replied, lost in her own thoughts. She knew him. She closed her eyes, the cold air from the door on her face. She took a deep breath. She could smell him. The scent was known to her and it made her feel sick. He smelled of dirt, blood, and death. Her eyes flashed opened. The other wolf, the one who had killed so many in the past few weeks and almost killed her. He was here in her home. She immediately started to shake so she moved to the counter to steady her posture. She turned to look at him.

"I feel like I know you," Emily stuttered.

"I have one of those faces." The man smiled.

Her eyes shifted to his mouth for only a moment. His smile grew bigger.

"And such an adorable face it is." Kari circled around the counter to join Devon. He now stood directly on the other side from Emily.

"Ignore them, they have been lovey-dovey all evening."

Emily felt Christina's hand on her own, warm to the touch. Still she stared.

"Kari tells me you were in an accident recently, are you healing well?" Devon questioned. His smile was so big it made it look as if his face was going to crack.

"I will live," she replied quickly. The .357 was not far away from her thoughts.

"So, ladies and gents, what do we have planned for this evening?" Devon questioned, with a big tooth-bearing grin that drew Emily's eyes back to his mouth.

She could smell the stench of decay from his breath.

"Alcohol, much consumption of alcohol," Jake called out.

Both Christina and Kari replied with a squeal of excitement, but Emily only stared at the intruder in her home. The intruder into her life—the one who almost took it from her—and now she knew his face. The shaking had stopped, but she took a big, deep breath to calm her emotions. She wanted to attack—to be the *other her*—and rip his throat out with little worry about who saw.

"Mi casa es su casa," she stuttered. Emily looked from Devon to Kari who now hung on his arm. She took another deep breath stepping back, but did not get far, bumping into Christina. She turned glaring at the other woman. She had not noticed it before, but the woman was much taller than she was. Christina's dark brown eyes looked down on her and she smiled.

"What is your poison of choice?" Emily heard someone ask, and turned to see Jake pulling glasses from the cupboard. "We brought tequila, vodka and Mr. Jack Daniel's is also in the house." He began opening bottles one at time.

"Tequila," Emily stated, feeling a hand on her side as Christina hugged against her. It would have been something that drove her crazy before—the invasion of personal space from someone she had just met—but right now, she could only think about the man across from her, as he stared and smiled her way with unknown intentions. She looked as an ice-filled glass was set in front of her, quickly downed it, and looked from Jake back to Devon.

She felt the chill of the November night air across her legs and arms and looked back to see the door still open. She pulled away from Christina who hesitated to release her position. Emily crossed the room shutting the door, her back against the wood frame, and took a deep breath. All of their eyes were on her—a friend, two strangers, and *him*.

"Who is up for some pizza?" Kari held her phone high in the air to catch everyone's attention.

Emily glanced at the bedroom door taking another deep breath. "I think I am going to put on some clothes." She walked in the direction of the bedroom, but almost immediately, Jake was there with another drink.

"You look fine," Christina called out from the counter. She had just placed a glass of her own down. Emily quickly turned her own glass high until empty. A bit of tequila ran down her chin, and she quickly wiped it away.

"I will just be a moment," Emily said, circling past Jake.

Emily entered her room and did not slow, going for the gun. She opened the purse, pulled the .357 free from its holster, and stared at it intently. Something stopped her. She put the gun back in its place. She could hear the noise coming from the other room. She turned back and looked toward the door.

Devon—his big grin ever present—was leaning against the doorframe, casting a large shadow into the room. "If we are intruding we can leave, understand if you need your space with everything you have gone through."

"It is a little late to worry about being intrusive," she indicated.

"I suppose." He grinned. "There must be so much going through that pretty little head of yours. So many questions you want answered. But, now is neither the time nor the place for such a conversation, now is it? Not with your friends in the next room waiting for you."

"When is the time?" Emily questioned. She walked toward the foot of the bed and looked at the pants on the end. She had intended to wear them to the club and just never put them away.

"Soon, all things will come to you." Devon walked away.

Emily paused. She picked up the jeans from the floor, looking back to the bedside table. "Damn it," she muttered to herself, pulling the shorts down her legs, and just as quickly, pulling the jeans over her figure. The jeans filled with holes, bought whole and she shredded them to suit fashion by her own means. She rushed to the nightstand quickly tucking the gun into the rim of the pants.

They were toasting to something as she re-entered the living room and picked up the bottle of cherry brandy, pouring herself a drink. "A toast to new friends, adventures, living life…and questions answered." She did not wait for any of the others to say a word as she downed her drink.

Emily set her glass down; she got a suggestive nod from Devon, who also took a drink. She then glanced at Kari, who seemed to be in the middle of a dance, lost to her own music. Did her friend know the man she was with? "So Kari, Devon, so serious after just meeting each other?"

Kari immediately came back to attention and smiled, peering from Devon to Emily. "Isn't he wonderful?"

"He is something," Emily replied.

"Tell me Emily, if this is not too personal, how do you feel knowing you are the lone attack survivor when so many have died from the animal attacks?" Jake questioned, and immediately got a smack on the arm from Christina.

"I just hope they catch and put the animal down." Emily poured another drink. She knew she needed to get him alone.

"Here, here." Christina lifted her glass.

Devon glared at both of them, but his smile did not change. Emily took another shot putting her glass back on the counter. She turned, stepping into the living room, only stopping once she reached the small entertainment center in the lone corner of the room. She turned on the radio, blasting music into the home.

Emily had almost forgotten about the fourth woman in the house. Melissa sat alone on the couch, a drink in front of her. She shared a shy smile as their eyes met. She crossed the room stopping at the counter picking up the waiting shot.

The music was of some Celtic variety. Kari rushed past grabbing Christina by the wrist and taking her into the living room where they began to dance. Jake followed suit, but only to watch the two women.

Emily sat back on her stool and eyed Devon. "Life is funny sometimes. I feel lucky to be alive, and everyone keeps reminding me of just how lucky I am."

"You truly are." Devon made no attempt to hide his devilish smile.

"So, I was just another *victim*." Emily poured a shot—the final shot—from her bottle.

"A chance happening. You were at the wrong place at the wrong time," he replied, leaning into the counter.

Their faces were so close she could taste his breath—the smell of liquor and death was so strong that she felt her stomach churn.

"So full of your own self-worth, you think you are special?"

"Just lucky an old drunk happened by," Emily stated, taking her shot, she never attempted to move away from him. "And now?"

"Nothing more than an inconvenience, something to toy with." Devon leaned away to take a shot of his own.

"So you intend on finishing what you started?" Emily questioned with a stone-cold glare, her lip twitched in horror and fear.

"I just haven't decided on what to do with you yet...let you experience the true nightmare to come? If you think the seizures are painful, wait until the first full transformation."

"And the other options?"

"For me or you?" He laughed. He glanced at the others. "I am sure you would be a fun fuck for a couple of nights before the turn, but after…nothing worse than a bitch in heat. I could help you transition, but then I would never know if you could make it through on your own, or if you were worthy of having me take you. If that were the case, I would rip out your throat out. Be done with it. A thrilling climax to it all, for me anyways."

They took a shot in unison and resumed looking into each other's eyes, neither blinking.

"The end result is all the same. I hunt and I kill. I've been doing it my whole life. You are nothing more than someone's experiment."

"There are others?" Emily questioned.

Again, Devon glared off behind her to the others and then back into her eyes.

The thought of there being others never occurred to her. But of course, there were others out there. Her luck wasn't that terrible—for her to come across the only werewolf in existence.

"Some. Very territorial and even closer than you think," Devon replied. "There was another here, but I took care of him before I began my hunts. But that is enough about the hunt…we have other things to discuss."

"Like what?" She leaned forward. She could almost taste his lips they were so close.

"The hunger. It is in you, I can smell it. I can also smell them—the cattle—but more importantly, I can smell the one who has been inside you." Devon smiled. "I took care of the other—the pretty boy. He was a fun hunt and so easy to get in the wilderness all alone. The other one though, he is a hunter. I can smell it on you. He is different from all other meat. He has a kindred soul of sorts. It would be more interesting if it were him I had bitten. More joy for someone like me."

"You leave Colin out of this." Emily bit her lip, raising her voice a little too loud, but the others never heard.

"He has a name." Devon smirked. "I assume he knows what you are now? I mean, he can probably taste the predator on your lips with each kiss. The hunger in your sweat… I could even smell his blood when I kissed your hand."

Emily pulled away from him for a moment, looking to her hands on the counter.

"Then there is your little friend."

Emily instantly turned, looking back at Kari and the others—who seemed to be having fun in the other room, and then back to Devon.

"Not her, the other. The little Indian. I can smell her native blood on the air in here. Mutts are sweet, their blood intoxicating. I am sure her screams will be delicate and delicious. I may even turn her. I am sure she can be dominated."

Emily continued to bite her lip.

"These other three, they have no meaning to you…even the little bitch. You could care less in comparison to the hunter and lesbian. You don't have to worry though. They will wait until after your big change. I mean, I could never take away from you the feeling of killing one of those closest to you."

"I won't…I will not," Emily quickly announced.

"We will see," Devon stated with a big grin. "Turn, look at them," Devon nodded in the direction of the other four. "Can you smell it? Can you hear it?"

"What?" Emily questioned looking at the others. His next words were a whisper in her ear, how he moved around the counter so swiftly she did not know. She could feel his warm breath.

"The little minx, Kari, lustful and in heat…I can smell her from here—all hot and bothered and ready to go. Don't look with your eyes—you have other senses, very powerful ones. Scent is the one you will find a new love of. The black woman, Christina, I can hear her heartbeat from here and how it beats ever so swiftly when she looks at Jake—and he is so oblivious, doesn't even notice. Melissa…the wall-flower's still there on the couch, so close, but yet so far from the others," Devon stated, placing an arm on Emily's wrist. "You can smell it all, can't you; you can hear their hearts, their deep breaths. Now, think about how they will taste…"

Emily felt his hand glide up under her tank top and caress her left side where the bite wound he'd left was.

"I can still taste you," he whispered. "Sweet, and aged just perfect, tender and juicy." His tongue slipped past his lips and touched her ear. She was too terrified to move, frozen much like the first time they had met. "My mouth waters just at the thought of having you—having you completely. Animalistic, if just the once… before I taste your blood again."

Emily broke away from him. She felt his fingernails dig into her flesh as she moved, but was too shocked to say a word. She walked to the door of the house and stepped out into the night air. She shut the door behind her, but heard it creep open almost instantly.

Devon stood with his fingers in his mouth. "Tastes like strawberries." He pulled the door closed behind him.

"I want you to fucking leave." Emily turned to face him. She held a hand on her stomach.

"Or you will what?" Devon questioned. "Tell the others I'm… wait…*we*… are werewolves? They pity you now for what happened to you. Such a declaration will make all of them think you are crazy, which is the reason you haven't said anything already." Devon stepped up to her lifting his hands in the air between them. Emily was horrified to see his fingers, and the long fingernails she knew were not there before. He ran a nail across his cheek until it bled. He pushed his hand forward. "You know you want a taste."

His finger only inches away; she could not resist taking it into her mouth, her lips clasped around the hard joint. She could feel the tip of his nail on her tongue as he slowly pulled it away.

"You like how it tastes—salty and sweet and a touch wild. You are in heat, little bitch, and you have no idea how amazing the sex is when you have all your senses at your disposal. Every sinfully electric touch…they are so explosive that just one could drive you over the edge. And now, you have no control. You hate me for every breath I take, but your brain has no control over the rest of your body." He stepped forward and reached out, placing his hand on her lower back and pulling her close.

She could feel erection through his jeans. His free hand roamed up her stomach and finally rested on her throat, where she knew he could feel the pounding of her heart.

"I could take you inside and have my way with you in front of the others and you could not stop me. Your brain would yell for you to wake up from the erotic dream you were in, but your body would refuse to listen—enjoying ever thrust of the animal within us, doing as we can—as we must to survive. Why don't you stop me? I can see it every time you open your eyes…you want me dead. Yet, you are too weak…"

Emily thrust her hands forward into his chest pushing him away several steps before he stopped moving. "I do have control," she said harshly, her breath heavy as if she had just finished a marathon. She glanced around her neighborhood with a worried and terrified expression.

"You do have some fight in you." Devon laughed, stepping forward and running a finger across her cheek before he stepped past her. "Tell Kari I had a…emergency and I will be in touch."

Emily watched him walk down the sidewalk until he disappeared from sight. She paused when she saw the black Suburban, and the shadow of a figure inside. She knew immediately it had to be Detective Vance. She crossed her arms and walked back inside.

16

"MORNING, SLEEPING BEAUTY—or—I guess, Little Red Riding Hood is more fitting."

Emily rolled over.

Colin stood in the doorway of the bedroom, his voice had only been a whisper but enough to wake her.

"What…how did you get in here?" Emily looked around, noticing she was not alone in the bed. She never knew when her friend came in, let alone crawled into bed with her. Nor did she know, why she was in bed with her. Ashley had slept beside her.

"Your front door was wide open…" Colin raised his coffee cup in the motion of a toast. "I told you to lay low, spend the nights alone… not have some wild sex orgy at your home—or whatever the hell happened last night."

"What are you talking about?" Emily rolled off the bed. She was still in the black tank top and jeans. She stumbled from the bed walking toward the living room and immediately saw the covers in the floor in between her two couches. "Where is my end table?" she questioned, trying to ignore the four-people lying in a mass of covers and bodies. She ran her hand across her forehead and over her eyes.

"What time is it?" She struggled to remember anything that happened after Devon left.

"Oh, it must have been a good one." Colin laughed.

"Last thing I remember…" Emily paused, grabbing Colin by his arm dragging him toward the door in the process.

"What?" he questioned.

"He was here…"

"Who?" he asked.

"The other…wolf." She looked around, and in particular, in the direction of where the detective's vehicle had been sitting.

"Are you kidding me?" Colin questioned, turning away from her. "How?"

"Kari. He weaseled his way into her life and at the same time mine." Emily replied. She walked over to the small table outside of the door and sat down.

"What did he want?" Colin questioned, taking the other seat.

Emily leaned forward, looking down at the table before meeting Colin's eyes.

"He is toying with me, but he may have let something slip," Emily stated with an eager smile. "He said there was another wolf here…the first attack victim was not a random attack. It was another werewolf. Do you think you can find out who the first victim was?"

"It is all over the papers, but I have a friend…we can get some more information from him and go check it out." Colin took a sip of his coffee.

"It's all over the papers, but I have a friend…" Colin took a sip of his coffee, "we can get some more information from him and go check it out." He set his cup on the table.

Emily picked it up without hesitation and took a sip. "He's in control, Colin…this means I can control it too." She set it back down. Emily sat back in her seat as Colin reached forward to clasp his hand over hers. "Things don't seem quite as bleak as they did yesterday."

"I'll call you when I know something," Colin said, leaving Emily sitting outside.

EMILY COULD BARELY contain her anxiety, spending most of the day reading outside and avoiding others. Hours had passed when Colin finally called with an address for the first victim. He could not go with her but asked her to be careful.

She pulled her jeep up the long, winding driveway and brought it to a stop. The house was old and not well cared for. The exterior—white siding with aged paint—was in desperate need of sanding and being re-done. The doors swung freely in the wind, and the window screens were torn from age. She stepped up onto the screeching front porch and approached the aged oak door, scuffed from years of abuse.

Emily knocked three times and waited a minute before she did it again. "Hello," she called out. She took another glance around before walking to the back of the house.

There was an old greenhouse out back, the roof cracked letting the chilled elements in. "Hello," she called out again walking toward the swinging open door.

"Can I help you?"

She saw him through the blurred walls. A barrel-chested black man, standing well-over six feet four watched her. He wore a white t-shirt with suspenders that held his unbuttoned, shredded jeans up. His head and face were both clean-shaven; the only sight of hair was under his lower lip. Thin-rimmed glasses covered his eyes. He smiled for a moment when he saw her clearly.

"What can I do for you?" He rubbed his fingers with the dripping wet rag in his hand.

"Are you Max Erma?" Emily questioned.

"I'm Max," he replied. "Is there something I can do for you, miss? You have a face full of questions."

"I don't know how to ask this…I am here about your brother," Emily stated.

Max pulled his glasses away from his eyes with his plump fingers and smiled as he took a better look at her. "Miss, my brother passed weeks ago—a terrible thing that was. The funeral was short and sweet, just as he would have wished it. I recognize you from the papers, only survivor of the horrible attacks. So, I must ask, Red, are you here to pay your respects to my dearly departed brother? Or do you have the same…problem he had in life?" The man looked around as if to make sure there was no one else to hear his words. "You have the curse?"

"A living nightmare," she muttered. Emily lifted the left side of her white tank top to expose the bite wound.

"Nasty, nasty business, that is." Max turned, tossing the rag to the ground inside the old greenhouse. "It causes much wonder though, how did you know he was of the affliction?"

"Even nastier business." Her eyes darted to the ground between them.

"Ah, so you are the new hunt of choice. I am not going to lie to you, Red, I'm glad my brother died. He lived a hard life—one I do not wish on such a youngling as yourself." Max stepped toward her. "He is finally at peace." He walked past her. "Follow me; I am sure you have many questions. I can answer some…Johnny can answer the others."

Emily looked after the man with wonder…Johnny Erma was his deceased brother.

Max looked back at her. "Come on, Red, you must keep up we have a bit of ground to cover."

They walked past the house toward the wilderness behind. He picked up a long stick and never slowed—not even to look and see if she still followed—not once, as they walked nearly a mile through a wilderness trail, kept clear by foot travel. It was not until they topped the mountain that she saw the cabin—rugged, rough lumber outside, but it was almost beautiful in its setting—surrounded by trees in a small clearing, looking like a painting come to life.

As they approached the back of the cabin, she saw a generator and a large stack of firewood. The generator started on the second pull from the much larger man. Max turned to look at her—the man weighed at least three-hundred pounds, but showed no effect of the mile- walk up hill.

"Winded, Red?"

Emily shook her head no.

The large man laughed, pulling keys from his pocket. He approached the door, there was a knob, but a couple of padlocks kept the door from opening from the outside. He stepped inside and turned the lights on to the single room. Table, chairs, a fireplace and bed with lots of blankets, quilts and even a bearskin rug in front of the fireplace. It was almost romantic in its old lodge way.

"Me and my two brothers, we built this by hand. Carried all the material up that very path you just walked. Lots of blood sweat and tears went into these walls." Max laughed, looking around for a moment, before pulling a chest from a corner and opening it. He reached inside pulling out chains and tossing them to the floor between them. "I know you have questions and lots of them, but I have some for you first. When were you attacked?"

"The morning of October 19th," Emily replied.

Max paused as he seemed to contemplate what he was just told. "The same morning my brother died, very fitting he was targeted by this other. So, the night my brother died, you were born..." The large man laughed and the hearty sound echoed through the one-room cabin. "Means you have a short time to prepare."

"What do you mean?" Emily questioned, walking across the room and sitting at the table.

"You've had what two…maybe your third attack by now, right?" Max questioned, picking up a leather-bound notebook.

"You mean seizures?" Emily asked.

"Yes, the first knocked you out for hours, maybe even days. The second, you remembered, but it still knocked you unconscious for a number of hours. The third was the most painful according to my brother. The fourth happened around 28 days after the attack. It was the first time he turned." Max twisted the notebook string free placing it on the table between them. "My brother kept a journal from the night he woke after his attack. He was like that, all school and stuff and writing…but from that night, he always kept it at his side. It was nearly two years after his attack when I learned what he went through and what he was."

"Did he ever find a cure?" Emily questioned.

"Never looked…you see those chains there, Red." Max glanced back to the center of the room where the chains, leather straps, and padlocks were all in a crumpled pile. "He tried to fight it, but he found the longer he went without changing, the worse the eventual change was. And the less control he had….it cost us Baxter."

"Baxter?" Emily asked.

"Our oldest brother. Johnny had gone nearly three months, keeping the beast bottled inside…even got comfortable enough in his body he did not chain himself up. When the seizure happened, he changed and had no control over the animal. It killed our brother and he never forgave himself for that. And from then on, he would change twice a month. He wouldn't fight it, just let the change happen. He had control and they were almost painless transformations…but he never once let it happen without being chained here in this cabin."

"I have until…the 19th?" Emily questioned.

Max laughed a hearty laugh sending an uncomfortable chill racing down Emily's back. "I am no expert, Little Red, but I am betting sometime within the thirty-day mark of when you got that nasty little bite…give or take a few days. You will become something only spoke of in fairy tales and horror movies."

Emily reached forward opening the journal and looked at the first short entry.

> April 4th…Haven Hospital They are telling me I have been here for eleven days. They were even about to turn off the machines I am currently hooked to, family given me up for dead. Momma has not moved from my bedside, frail she sits in her wheelchair and cries when she can muster the water. I still don't remember what the hell happened to me.

Emily closed the book, looking up at Max.

He looked at the journal and not her. "If you don't intend on kil-lin' yourself, you can have that…"

Emily gave him a confused look.

"You have thought about it, haven't you?"

Emily glared at the large man who smiled back at her. He always seemed to be smiling.

"Brother tried twice in the first month but could never go through with it according to the journal," Max replied.

Emily opened the journal and looked over the first entry again for a moment before she looked up at Max. "Did you ever see it?"

"No! Part of me would have liked to have seen it…what he went through and not just read about it…but I fear I would have never thought of him as my brother from then on. Just a host to a thing…"

Emily lowered her head and no longer looked at him.

"How did you find out?" Emily questioned.

"At Baxter's funeral. Me and Johnny decided we needed to come up here and drink away our sorrow. It was his way of bringing me up here to confess it all. I thought he was drunk," Max replied.

"How did he get you to believe him?"

"I don't know if I ever truly did, until after his death and I came up here. He lived up here from then on out, small garden on top of this hill. Killing animals…almost a hermit's life. I brought him clothes, other food…gas…necessities. I had not been inside this cabin since that night of drinking, and then I saw the mess…and his journal."

Emily took a moment to glance around the room, everything looked rather neat and put in its place, but then she saw the claw marks in the walls of the cabin.

"I sat here by firelight and read that journal cover to cover—mul-tiple times—and then I accepted he was not crazy. The last entry is dated the day before the attacks."

Emily opened the journal scanning to the last page, through seven years' worth of entries until she saw a blank page and flipped back.

October 17th… I saw the young man again today. I should not have gone to town, I could smell him from a mile away. The stench of another wolf still stings my nose. A young man by appearance but I feel he is much older than his face projects. I've seen him three times now, in two different towns. He is following me. I don't know what he wants but I do hope he moves on soon. I feel I must change tomorrow. I can't trust keeping the beast locked away for much longer.

"I never even realized he was slipping off to town. There are nearly five hundred entries in there over a seven-year period, almost all about what he was going through," Max stated. "It is going to be dark soon, if you want I can build you a fire and you can stay the night here. I will be down the hill. Maybe it will help you understand what it was he went through, and what is going to happen to you."

Emily hesitated, holding the journal in one hand and her cell phone in the other. "Thank you. I will take you up on it." She stood leaving the journal at the table and walked outside to make a call.

"Hey, Colin. Don't worry about me. I will call you come morning. I think I did the right thing coming here and seeing Erma's family…there is a journal. The man kept a journal about what he went through, and his brother was kind enough to let me look through it…I will call you in the morning."

———————◆———————

HOURS PAST, THE fire had no problem heating the one-room cabin. Emily had not opened the journal since she reentered the cabin, she just paced the floors. She had removed her long-sleeve shirt, only wearing her tank top and jeans now. The cabin smelled, he had not noticed before. There was the smell of burning lumber, but the stench of fur was just as evident now.

Another growing pain hit Emily the moment the sun was down and the moon was in the sky—and the higher it advanced, the more she felt it in her stomach.

She stopped her restless pacing and stared at the table where she'd left the journal--it seemed to call to her. She walked the short distance and began to flip through the pages until she found the first entry a month after the attack.

May 1st...I felt it all day yesterday, that same sinking feeling in my stomach. As if I could not get enough to eat but at the same time I was full, a churning deep inside me. I knew what it was. I felt the same churn before. It was not until late in the day, the closer to dark it got it really dawned on me what was happening to me. The cold sweat, the feeling...so indescribable...I remember sitting down for dinner with Momma. She looks so frail I don't expect she will be with us much longer. I hope I am wrong and she outlives us all. I remember the cold look in her eyes as she stared at me and Max from across the table. It is so hard to get the three boys all at home at once, let alone down for a meal. But she seemed happy with just the two of us. I remember the beans, the almost soured taste...I loved Momma's beans. I don't think they will ever taste the same after that. I had to excuse myself from the table, got an odd look from the both of them. I went out to the greenhouse just trying to enjoy the warm air. I barely made it across the yard, stumbled I did. Twice I fell to the wet ground. Collapsed again at the door nearly tore it from the frame. I cried, I could not hold them back. I yelled for Max...Bax...Momma...even poor long-dead Dad...even turned to God himself. I remember screaming out to him. But no one would answer me. Only the blinding moonlight spoke to me. The pain, every muscle in my body stretched and pulled as if it was being torn from my skin...the bones they cracked...I could hear them bend and mold into something...inhuman. My eyes blurred, I could feel my own teeth grow as my jaw seemed to dislocate from its place. My entire face hurt as if someone was pushing in from both sides. My heart it pounded, up in my throat and eyes…every beat felt like a hammer to my chest. I have never felt such agony. I remember wanting to die. I woke what felt like a day later….but only an hour had passed since I excused myself from my Momma's table, Just one fucking hour was all it was…what is happening to me?

May 6th…I woke this morning in the woods behind the family home, I know the spot well the small pond me and my brothers used to catch bluegills and small bass from and roast them on an open fire. Those times seem so long ago now. So…Human. I was naked as a jaybird I swear I heard the chipmunks gasp as I stumbled back toward home. Covered in blood, mud and I am not even sure what the rest of the filth was. I was so confused at first how it was I got there…but I remember now. I remember staring into my own reflection in the pond and the wolf stared back at me.

May 8th…I turned again. I remember it all this time, the stalking of the deer and its newborn fawn…I don't think I'll ever want jerky again. The way I tore into the mother as the fawn watched in terror…it screamed almost human before I turned my claws and fangs on it too. I can't live like this. I can't be this monster.

June 3rd…We buried our mother this morning. I cried like an infant, but I am thankful. Thankful she will not know the thing I am. I feel the change coming on. It has been almost a month since I turned. I almost welcome the moon…

A cold sweat ran over Emily's body. She glanced to the fire still burning strong then turned and walked to the door, opening it to the outside. She dropped, sitting in the doorway. The cold airs beat against her face and bare arms. She glared up at the moon as it started to creep into the sky. Johnny Erma's journal was still open on the table behind her. Emily turned back and then again looked toward the outside darkness. She could see lights off in the distance from nearby towns—with no leaves on the trees it was easy to see a lot from such a high peak. She took in a deep breath of the fresh mountain air, watching the exhale of steam float off into the darkness. She repeated it several times. Everything Johnny wrote about, she felt, but she did not know if it was the 'power of suggestion' or it was actually happening. The knot in her stomach, the thump of her heart…it reminded her it was real. She could only think of the one advantage she had over Johnny at this point…she knew what was happening. She knew what she was going to become. If the both Johnny and Devon were able to overcome and control their other side…so could she.

Emily stood up from the doorway, crossing the room, only stopping for a moment to glare at the still-opened book. Picking it up she walked to the fireplace and took a seat on the bearskin rug. She randomly opened the book and began reading the page in front of her.

> March 23…One year to the night I was attacked and it is the first time I allowed the change to happen…even willed it. I made the excuse to leave town, go someplace far, far away. I drove for four hours and then hiked into the wilderness for two miles…far enough away from people. I can hunt…I can be the predator I think I was meant to be. This all had to happen for a reason. I hate to say this…I think I enjoyed it.

> I woke; clothing nearby….no one was harmed. I can beat this. I can control it…this does not have to be a curse!

Emily smiled as she set the book down on the rug, leaning back to enjoy the heat of the fire on her skin. She closed her eyes and took a deep breath. She could feel the growling inside her as she breathed. It was not just the power of suggestion…it was happening. She sat up, pulling the black tank top over her head and setting it on the floor beside her, lowering again to her back she raised her hips from the rug and unbuttoned her pants and pushed them down her thighs. She sat up, again, pulling them down her legs and setting them down beside the tank top. Wearing only red lace panties, bra and socks, she lay on the bearskin rug. The fur prickled her skin as she stretched out enjoying the heat. The pain was there, but it was nowhere near as bad as the journal described.

She arched her back as the pain intensified—it was almost pleasurable. Emily smiled. Her canines grew and her jaw extended to support her new teeth. She pulled at the rug, her body arching up from the floor until only her feet and shoulders touched it, and her physical frame seemed to extend.

"Amazing," a voice called out.

Emily never heard Max step into the room. As the shadow of the man engulfed her petite body, her eyes shifted in shape and color—taking on a yellow glow. Her fingers were longer now, with nails to match. She sat up, now fully conscious of the change. She twisted her head and glared at the fire and then her own hands. Her lips bared to show teeth as Max circled around, leaning in front of her, but out of reach.

She thrust her hand in front of her eyes and then glared into Max's.

"Do you hear me?" he questioned, leaning a little closer with his big smile. "You do, don't you, Red? I lied before. I really did want to see my brother's change. The very idea of such a thing being possible… maybe that is why the only time he tried to tell me he was so drunk he could not remember the next day and tried to ignore when I asked about it." Max smiled.

In an instant, she was in his face tapping her fingers on his cheek long nails extended. "Please…leave," she snarled. Max stumbled back. Emily leaned toward him growling. Max gasped in terror as he turned, running out the door.

Devon stepped in as Max ran out. He showed little worry about Max who was likely halfway down the trail by now. "Still a pup. You are days away from your first full transformation…and you're letting a perfectly good meal escape."

Emily took several steps back until she was against the wall.

"Where are you going? You have such control, but you still haven't turned completely."

Devon approached, and with every step he took toward her, the feral Emily took a step to one side or the other. He mocked her with his own movements. The hunt did not stop until she had crossed the entire floor of the one-room building. With her back to the wall, she stood and growled at him. Her clawed hand slashed at him but Devon was faster and he caught her wrist just inches away from his throat.

"You are a fighter—I can tell that about you now. It is not often I read someone so wrong. You are still slow and do not know how deadly you truly are." Devon stepped closer pressing his body into Emily's pinning her firmly against the wall at her back. Having effectively trapped her, he grabbed her other wrist to prevent her from launching another attack. "You may even be more of a threat than the other… we will know in a matter of days." He flashed his canines—which were larger than hers—lunged forward and it her growling lower lip until his teeth pierced the flesh and blood dripped from his sharp fangs. Devon pulled away, looked into her eyes and smiled…

Emily jerked her head forward swift and sudden, teeth breaking skin as she dug into the side of his neck. Blood spilled from the wound and he released his grip on her wrists and pulled away, whirling in pain and shock. "Bitch," he called out. Emily made for the door and the freedom of darkness.

17

EMILY WOKE. A terrified and confused look on her face pulling her way from the body of the hollow tree, soaked in rotted bark, mud and blood as it clung to her naked flesh. She trembled from shock, and the chill of a frosty fall morning that bit at her toes. She looked up the hill before her at the long path she could see cutting through the mountainside. Slowly, with her arms across her chest she walked up the trail, bare feet hindering her progress.

She walked cautiously. Reaching the peak, she tried, but could not pick up Devon's scent. From the top of the hill she could see the cabin just a short walk away. Her heart beat faster and faster with each step. She glanced up at the cabin. The door still wide open. "Are you in there?" Emily questioned aloud, looking to the sky and the sun as it peaked over the horizon. She took several steps forward…still no answer. With a sigh of relief, she walked past the threshold and inside.

"You gave me quite the scare last night."

Jolted, Emily spun around and saw Max sitting by the blazing fire with a shotgun across his lap. "But I deserved as much, Red. I wanted to see it…" His eyes drifted up and down her filthy naked frame before he looked back to the fire.

"I thought he had got you…"

"I high tailed it, Red—straight to my truck. Spent the night at a motel half an hour away from here, didn't return until daylight." He laughed, glancing her way.

Emily grabbed a blanket to cover her body.

"He won't stop…until you're dead or his." Max stood, putting the shotgun on his shoulder. "I put a card on the inside of my brother's journal, if I can be of any help to you, Red, don't be afraid to call."

Emily watched until the large man was gone, and smiled. She'd had some control the night before, and he was evidence. There was no care in it as she dressed as quickly as she could, stuffing the bra and panties into pockets anxious to leave the cabin. Emily hastily grabbed the journal only stopping for a moment at the door, a glance back to the chains before she headed toward the trail.

Emily walked slowly down the path…at first. The farther she moved, the faster she moved, and the less cautious she became. As she rounded the Erma's house, she jogged the last bit to her vehicle. Quickly climbing inside, she closed her eyes and took a deep breath. She started the engine with her eyes still closed, then glanced down at the journal in her lap. Noticing the red smudge on the cover, she quickly opened it, On the front page, over Johnny's handwriting, and written in blood were the words: *See you soon!*

Her heart raced as she pulled off in a hurry to get home.

———————◆———————

A MILE FROM the Erma residence, blue lights came from nowhere blinding Emily. She glared into her rearview mirror. The moment she saw the black Suburban she knew who it was. She watched as Detective Vance stepped from her truck and slowly walked toward the passenger side of the vehicle. Emily could feel her heart pound harder the closer the other woman got. She passed the passenger door and paused, her gun drawn.

"Shut your engine off," Vance called out.

Emily did as she requested.

"Step from the vehicle with your hands in the air,"

Emily did not look at the woman directly, but at her hands positioned out in front of her wielding her weapon.

Emily opened the door stepping out into the cold morning air. She was freezing, her feet were soaked, and she still felt the chill of walking naked in the forest frost.

"Walk around to this side of the vehicle, Ms. Meyer."

"What is this about, Detective Vance?" Emily questioned, holding her arms above her head, she started to walk.

"An anonymous tip, Ms. Meyer. You were involved in a murder," Vance replied, taking a step away from the hood as Emily rounded the front. "Hands on the hood."

Emily did as she asked.

"Eyes forward."

Emily looked at the black hood of her car and she could see her own reflection…still muddy and covered in dry blood.

"Whose blood is that?" Vance demanded, still with her gun drawn.

Emily looked at her reflection with dismay.

"On your knees, Ms. Meyer, hands behind your back."

Emily did not reply. Her chest pounded as if with each beat her heart was going to explode from her body. The sudden pain in her stomach caused her to double over onto the hood, but it was not just due to the stomach pain. Vance had grabbed an arm and swiftly pulled it behind her body.

"I can explain," Emily called out, feeling her skin crawl.

"Another animal attack I am sure." Vance twisted the other arm, slapping the cuffs around Emily's wrists. "You have gotten away with almost two dozen murders…somehow hiding them as animal attacks."

Emily never felt the hit, her vision went blurry and then silence.

———————◆———————

EMILY'S HEAD POUNDED. Blood, thick and sticky, had dried to her face. Her arms held tight in a wooden framed chair by double set of cuffs, her wrist twisted and bruised from the awkward tight shackles. "I can explain," she muttered. She could only see out of one eye, the other obstructed with matted hair.

"Really. I would like to hear the explanation for the deaths of twenty-one people—that is the current count of unexplained animal attacks here in West Virginia alone since the night of your so-called attack. Three others in Kentucky…twenty-four people murdered by you,"

Emily could not see the other woman but knew she was close, the sound of her voice almost a whisper in her ear. Even though Vance talked low and delicate it caused her head to throb with each word.

"Where are we?" The room was dark; only a single light hung from the ceiling directly above her head, and it swung from side to side casting shadows all around her. The floors were wooden, old and not cared for. She could tell nothing else about her cell, but it was obvious they were not at the police station.

"You have put me in a…delicate situation, Ms. Meyer. See I know what you are. You are a murderer. A cold-blooded killer…but everyone else sees you as just a lucky victim," Vance replied. "And I admit to being overzealous…I should take you in, the proof is all over your body. I am sure we will find your most recent victim in the coming days. I just cannot decide what to do with you…"

Emily took a deep breath and wheezed as she exhaled.

"You have nothing to say for yourself?"

Emily could now see Vance as she approached not stopping until she kneeled in front of her. She was dressed down; jeans and boots, long-sleeve shirt, but the most noticeable thing about the outfit was the latex gloves. "Just admitting to one murder is only going to piss me off. I want to know about them all. And I'm not the person you want to piss off at the moment."

* * *

EMILY WOKE, STILL tied to the chair…now on its side on the cold floor. The lingering headache only intensified as she struggled to move and breathe.

"I was beginning to worry I might have hit you too hard."

From her awkward position on the floor, Emily could only see Vance's feet.

"I don't understand…how does a woman with your privileged upper middle-class upbringing become a serial killer? And such a damn good one at that. You have everyone fooled. Hell, if you had not faked your own accident no one would even know who you are. And you sure as hell would not be a suspect." The ringing of a phone interrupted her from speaking. "You have so many people fooled; Colin has called you twice; your mom and dad have each called once; someone named Kari has called once, as well—I don't know her; And, here we are, for the seventh time…Ashley. That girl must really be worried about you. Do any of them know what kind of monster you are?"

"How long…?" Emily twisted, she was in a lot of pain—not all of it was from the head trauma.

"How long what? How long have you been out? Let's see—" Vance looked at her watch. "Fourteen hours. As I said, I did not think you were ever going to wake up."

"It is dark outside—I'm not supposed to change again…" Emily struggled against her bonds and the chair.

"Change? Your kind cannot change. You are sick and should be put down like a dog," Vance said.

"You…have…your chance…" Emily began to spasm, her eyes changed color, and Vance immediately noticed.

"What is happening to you…?" The detective quickly sat up.

"You are—I am sick…" Emily continued to fight, twisting as her chest arched from the chair. "I am sorry…"

"…the fuck…" Vance rushed into the light kneeling down beside Emily.

"…should…have…taken…me…in." The wooden chair snapped. Emily brought her hands around in front of her—the cuffs still dangling at her wrists. She pushed her upper body off the floor. Her face was hidden by her hair. Vance reached forward, pushing it away to look at her.

Emily saw the horror in her reaction and smiled, showing her long canines. Vance fell to the floor, dropping her gun in the process.

"What the hell are you…?" Vance questioned, trying to get away.

"It said…I would not turn…not until a month had passed." Emily's once polite voice was gone—a hoarse monotone echoed through the room. Her body twisted as she fell into a fetal position.

Emily heard the Vance's breath, and then her footsteps. A moment later she felt the cold touch of a hand on her shoulder. Emily jolted at the touch. She was on top of Vance before the detective could reach for her misplaced gun. Wrapping her long thin skeletal fingers around her neck, she pinned Vance to the floor. "You really should not have pissed me off."

Vance struggled against her, but Emily held her down with her unnaturally bent legs across her waist. One hand at Vance's throat while the other held both wrists tight over her head, Emily glared into her eyes.

Vance spit in her face. "Fuck you."

The first swipe sliced her jugular, the second plunged into her stomach—both so quickly that Vance could not react. Instantly, the detective paled as she squirmed but she did not have the life left in her to even crawl.

Emily stood over her victim. "I am a monster…and I accept it now. I am in control—" She attacked again, slashing and slicing with her inhuman claws, cutting into the dead detective's back. Blood splattered, organs ripped and bones broke. She paused to look at her blood-soaked hands before attacking again, letting her anger control her.

EMILY LET THE hot water run over her skin. It was the third shower in as many hours. She waited just long enough for the water to get good and hot before she dove back in, and still she could not get clean. She could still see Vance's blood on her skin. Each time she closed her eyes, she saw Detective Vance…begging for her life, even though she never actually had a chance to do so, before the wolf tore her apart. She had walked for nearly an hour before she was finally picked up by a coal truck driver. The man gave her a lift only a couple miles from her own vehicle.

It was nearly dark now, a full night after she killed. She had control with Max—had she had any with Vance? Did she want to kill her? Part of her—a lot of her—wanted to kill the cop who treated her like anything but the victim she was. "Bitch!" she yelled out, water spilling into her mouth. "Why couldn't you just take me in." As many tears fell from her face as water droplets fell from the shower.

"You enjoyed it and you know it." The words came as a whisper on the air, in the detective's voice. Emily glanced out from her position in the shower. She was in a hotel room, two hours from home. She was running away…away from the possibility of hurting her friends or family. Away from Devon—who would likely follow her to the end of the world. Most importantly, she was running from herself and what she had become.

"You could not just leave me alone. You had to be a hero," she continued to talk aloud, bordering on a yell, her voice harsh. "You are dead, and I killed you. I did not want to kill anyone. This is not my fault." She quickly turned off the water. Soaking wet she stepped from the shower, placing her hand on the sharp-ridged railing and sliding it down. Blood spilled from the cut on her palm; she pulled away from it fast, but only looked at the now open wound. "It is not my fault…not my fault." She lashed out, shattering the mirror and it echoed through the room. Emily stood looking down at the shards of shattered glass and her own broken reflection. "None of this is my fault," she muttered in a soft voice. Blood dripped from her palm to the floor. Emily could now hear the sound of her phone in the other room. Again. It was the fifth time since she had checked into her room. "Leave me alone!" She walked until her wet back bumped into the sink, and she slid to the floor where she sat crying, face in her hands.

The loud crashing against the door broke her from her crying. She looked out into the other room of the hotel, and she could almost see as the door shake as someone knocked. A growl escaped her throat before she could act; her hand quickly covered her mouth to muffle the sound. "Coming," she called out. She grabbed the towel from its hanger and tiptoed around the glass on the floor. She pulled the bathroom door closed behind her. She wrapped the towel around her chest and could feel the draft of wind under it as she walked.

The man on the other side was no more than twenty and wore his hotel uniform.

"Miss, is everything ok?" He had short, wavy black hair, a hint of a shadow from an uneven beard. He smiled the moment he saw her and his eyes twitched in an attempt to look at her without being obvious.

"I am so sorry, I cut myself," Emily said in a soft voice, turning her hand to one side, showing the young man.

"I can get a bandage for you," he said with a mischievous grin, biting on his lower lip with a more obvious attempt at looking over her wet cleavage.

"My eyes are up here." She waved her bloody palm in front of her breast and then to her face.

"I am sorry ma'am…do you want that bandage?" he questioned with a schoolboy grin.

"Yes, please. And don't call me ma'am." She turned, walking toward her bed. She had hardly taken a seat on the harsh, uncomfortable mattress, when the young man was, again, back at the door. He had run the entire way to the hotel's office—which was just three doors down. He entered the room, looking around to see if there was anyone else.

"I am alone. You can shut the door," Emily stated, her wet legs crossed on the bed watching him approach.

He shut the door, turning back with a big smile that he tried to hide. He walked toward her, still looking around the room in an attempt not to look directly at her. He was close enough to touch. He took her hand in his, wiping the wound clean. A moment later shortly followed by the bandage and tape around her hand.

"All better?" he questioned, still with the schoolboy grin.

She grabbed the edges of his shirt and pulled him closer until she was able to taste his breath—and then she kissed him. It was slow and wet. She felt his hands run up her still-wet legs before she pushed him away.

"Not today kid," she said showing teeth.

"Did you just growl?"

She sat up smiling just as her phone began to ring, but she made no movement to get it from the opposite edge of the bed.

Emily paused, looking to the phone behind her. She glanced back at him in time to catch his eyes looking at her wet legs, his hands still there just below the towel. She looked toward the big window. I was growing dark outside.

"It is going to be dark soon…"

She got no reply as the young man's eyes drifted down her body.

"I'm no boy," he replied after his hesitation.

"Trust me, you are." She growled.

Again, her phone started to ring…

"Jealous boyfriend?"

She heard him mumble. Emily looked to the phone and it stopped, but only for a second before it started ringing again. She leaned back in the bed and grabbed the phone, looking at the caller ID—Ash.

"You need to leave…before you get hurt."

"I can handle it…you won't hurt me," the young man quickly responded, his eyes back on her legs.

"Trust me kid, you want to leave this hotel room before I get… excited." She showed no expression as she stood, crossing around him back to the door. Emily did not move until he was out. She watched him walk away. Every few steps he would glance back, hoping for her to recall him, but instead she looked to the sky, and the moon as it crept over the distant hills. She quickly shut the door and went to get her clothes. She had gotten rid of her socks and the bloodstained over shirt. Only the black tank top, jeans and underwear remained from the previous day's wardrobe. She was starting out the door when the phone rang again.

"Hello," she answered, just as the second ring started.

"I did not think you would ever answer, pup."

She did not have to ask who it was on the other end.

"If you have hurt her, I will kill you. I will rip your throat out."

"Still breathing and unscratched," he replied.

She started to pace. She could hear the laughter in his voice.

"I wanted to let you know I have the little bitch. And, you best turn your perky, little tail around and wag it back to town. I will call you with a time and place in two days. We will end this—wolf to wolf."

Only silence remained on the other end of the call.

Emily collapsed to her knees and elbows. The anger engulfed her. The shift was coming. She took a deep breath and arched her head up in the air, then breathed in as she fell to her side. "I am in control…"

EMILY AWOKE WITH the open journal in her hand. She looked around the room. She could see light peeking in through the window from the outside. It was the next day. She took a moment looking around for her phone. It was there, on the floor where she had collapsed. Emily quickly reached for it and called for Ashley, only getting voice mail. "Son of a bitch."

She dialed another number. "Colin, listen, I will be home in around three hours. I need you to come over."

The drive home felt like forever to her, she continued to watch everything in her rearview, half expecting a cop pull her over at any time. Images of her murdering Detective Vance continued to flash in her mind. She pulled into her drive, leaving the vehicle outside of the garage. She rushed into the house, leaving the door open.

In her room, she began to strip and changed into similar clothing to what she had been wearing, only clean. Bra, panties, a pair of cargo pants with multiple baggy pockets, and a long-sleeve, hunter green over top. She pulled her hair back into a ponytail as she exited the room. Colin was just walking into the house. She never even acknowledged him as she entered the kitchen. She walked up to the counter, opening drawers, and began to shift through her silverware, out of frustration she pulled the drawer from the cabinet, scattering its contents all over the floor.

"Hello to you too," Colin said, taking a seat on the counter. "A lot of people are really worried about you. You should not just disappear like that. I even drove by that address I gave you and saw nothing the next day. You were supposed to call me."

Emily glared at him. She left the room, only to return a moment later with Johnny Erma's journal in hand. She tossed it on the counter in front of him.

"This the journal?" Colin questioned.

"No, it's a cookbook, what do you think." She circled back to the other side of the counter, and began looking through her drawers and the cabinets, again.

"No reason to get testy." Colin pulled the journal over in front of him.

She looked up from her kneeled position. She could not contain it, she knew she was growling.

He stepped away from the stool and took several steps back into the living room. He glanced outside to the daylight, and then back to Emily.

"You have no idea how fucked up things have become in a few short days, Colin. I love you, and your sense of humor…but now is the time for you to button it up." She made a motion across her lips, her furious expression never changed.

"You just growled at me…" Colin said in a slightly high-pitched voice.

"Trust me, it could be worse." She opened the cabinet where pots and pans had been stored and began to pull stuff to the floor.

"Emily…talk to me," Colin spoke up. He was again at the stool, leaning over to see what she was doing. "What has happened?"

Emily rested her head for a moment, and then glared at him while walking to the cabinet. She gave him a scowl, lips parted as she was trying to find the words. She could see how nervous he was, like a rabbit ready to bolt.

"Detective Vance," Emily stated, looking away from Colin. "She pulled me over, Colin…took me to some barn and tried to make me confess to all the killings."

"Are you serious? How did you get away?" Colin questioned, with a pause.

Emily stood away from the counter, turned to leave the room.

With her back to Colin when she spoke, "I didn't….the wolf did. I gave in. And Colin…I enjoyed it. Fuck me. I enjoyed the feeling it gave me. And you want to know the fuck all of it? He has Ashley. The bastard has Ashley. That is why I came back here. I was over two hours from this place and going farther. I planned on just driving until I could not drive anymore, Colin. Getting away…from hurting the people I care for—and maybe leading him away from here. But he wants me here." Emily turned, her eyes were a shade of yellow, her pupils dilated and wild. "He wants to kill me or me to kill him…I don't know if I can kill him. Devon. The bastard deserves to die. But I don't know if I can do it…"

"You will…but you won't be alone," Colin proclaimed.

"What may happen if I do kill him….and in the blood lust… what if I kill you or Ashley?" Emily questioned, stepping backward getting farther away from Colin. "I cannot handle it."

"You won't. We need to worry about this creep and how we are going to take care of him. How long do we have?" Colin questioned, trying to look away from her eyes but unable to resist.

"He will call me tomorrow. For a meeting…"

"Then we have some time. I will call you in a bit," Colin replied, backing away from the counter before leaving the house.

19

EMILY DRESSED IN a spaghetti-strapped, maroon top and dark cargo pants, and matching maroon shoes. Her bloodshot eyes were covered by thick glasses to hide the dark circles. She had been crying since Colin left her home, and she knew her pupils did not look human. She could not control it. She fought the urge to growl at ever passing person—whether they proved to be a threat or not. The wolf wanted out.

Illyania Knox pulled the chair out from across from her. "We could have met in my office."

"I can't sleep…"

"Nightmares again?"

"No." Emily looked at the coffee. "I lay awake at night. I pace the room. I run on the treadmill trying to reach some level of exhaustion so I can sleep… and nothing seems to work."

"Where have you been?"

"What?"

"For the past few days, I've been in contact with your father."

Emily smirked. She was no older than ten when she saw her parents argue, it was the most intense argument they ever had. It was all due to Illyania Knox and her father. It was never clear whether they had an affair or not. Her mom had never spoken about it since. Emily held her breath for a moment.

"A police detective—Hastings—also came by looking for you, Emily. Where have you been?"

"I needed some space. I needed to get away from people looking over my shoulder every breath I took. It feels like the world is so small now, and I just want to run. I want to sleep—can you help me with that or not?" Emily questioned. She had a plan. She had packed two bags of clothing, and some memories—all sitting in the backseat of her jeep. She was going to save Ashley, and then run. She had a day, at least, before Devon would call. She needed a good night's sleep. She needed her wits about her. She needed to be in control of the wolf when she released it.

"You will call me if you have nightmares, again right?"

Emily watched the woman fill out a prescription for sleep medication. "Yes."

Knox handed her the prescription before she stood and left. Emily took a long deep breath.

❖

EMILY RETURNED HOME to find the Suburban waiting as she pulled into the driveway. She was barely out of the car when she saw Detective Hastings walking up to meet her. "Ms. Meyer."

"Detective. I was told you were looking for me?" Emily questioned.

"It is about my partner," Hastings announced. "Can we talk inside?"

"Sure." Emily walked on, she knew this could be a mistake. She opened the door, letting the much taller man walk through in front of her. She took a deep breath before following.

"You haven't seen Detective Vance, have you?"

"Not since the day here with you, no," Emily lied. She could feel her heart racing, the image of a bloody, mangled Vance flashed in her mind.

"She was put on leave recently."

"Really?"

"Medical reasons, but I wanted to check in on you in case she paid you a visit."

She watched him take a seat on the couch. "Care for a drink? you really look like you could use it."

Hastings smiled.

Emily set her keys on the table, quickly retrieving a couple of beers from the fridge before she returned, setting them on the table in front of him. "You partner didn't like me much." Emily watched the man twist the top off of one bottle and hand it back to her, before taking the other for himself.

"Messy divorce. Honestly, the day we came by here the first time, she said you reminded her of the woman her husband was leaving her for."

Emily frowned. "Sorry for her, but how could she have believed I killed all those people? I was laid up in a hospital bed for some of the murders...including Troy's."

"Something one of the nurses told her. She kept hanging onto how your coma was unexplainable—no medical reasons why you weren't awake."

Emily scowled. "Really." She took a big drink of her beer, watching the much older man do the same. There was a boyish quality to him, his face clean-shaven, but his hair was a mess even short. "Tell me, Detective, are you married?"

"Divorced." He held his left hand up for her to see.

It didn't matter. She felt the wolf. It wanted out—to let her emotions and feelings run wild. It wanted him. She was not going to give in. She stood up and walked back to the counter.

"I think you should leave."

She felt him looming over her. She turned to face him, just as he lifted his hands to remove her glasses. She immediately shut her eyes.

"Why are you hiding your eyes?" he questioned.

She heard him set the glasses on the counter. "Just light sensitive right now." She could smell his cologne. It was only making the hunger grow. She wanted him, as badly as she had wanted Colin the other night.

"You are lying, why?"

Emily took a deep breath opening her eyes, she knew they were bloodshot, but at least now, she hoped her pupils were normal. "Happy?'

"I am sorry." Hastings took a step back away from her.

Emily stepped forward. She had begun to breathe heavier, feeling the lust for the detective building. "I need you to leave."

"I am sorry," he said again, turning away from her.

She wanted to reach out, touch his shoulder…kiss his neck. "I hope you find your partner."

The detective stopped.

Emily sighed. She needed him to leave.

"You saw her, didn't you?" He turned, moving his coat to expose the pistol on his hip. His hand rested there, though she did not see it, she heard him click the button, freeing it from the guard.

"I did." She stepped forward closing the distance between them.

"When?"

Emily was close enough now. She placed her hands behind her back. This was control, she could feel her fingernails extending and she grimaced from the pain they caused. "Yesterday morning." She twisted her head and gritted her teeth through the pain.

"And?"

"She threatened me." Emily felt it, the growling pain in her stomach. It was no longer lust, but anger, driving her toward the detective. One foot after another…she was close, but still he did not pull his weapon. "She pulled me over. Wanted to know where I was going. She threatened to take me in—even frisked me—but then let me go."

"Where was this?"

"Few miles from here," she lied. She knew she could not tell him where, it would only be a matter of time before Vance's vehicle and body were found. And Emily needed time to save Ashley.

Hastings took his hand off the pistol, allowing the coat to close. "If you hear from her again, you call me."

Emily knew the detective was questioning everything she had told him. "I will." She watched him leave and carefully closed the door behind him. She was regretting coming home now. She pulled the prescription from its bag and headed to bedroom.

———◆———

EMILY REMEMBERED FALLING to sleep—curled up in her bed, thanks to the pills she had been prescribed. So, she knew this was a dream. She wore a long, flowing skirt that stretched to her ankles, with a matching long-sleeve, silk top. Before her was an erect wooden tepee stretching high above her. The moon was full and gave her a growing sensation of hunger mixed with anger. Smoke escaped the top of the rim of the structure, and even from the outside, she could feel the heat as it escaped the wooden slabs. She pushed her red mane off her shoulders as she slowly approached.

Emily moved through the thick skin cover over the door. The heat almost knocked her down as she entered, and small sweat beads immediately began to rise on her forehead. It did not feel like a dream, but she knew it was. The inside was made of three large circles, an outside ring, a step down to another, and then a third, where a circle of hot rocks caused steam to erupt into the air.

She took a deep breath, feeling her lungs fill with smoke, causing a new ache. Emily remembered Knox telling her how a deep sleep could cause more realistic dreams, but this was different than she was expecting. Another deep breath and she could feel herself growing more aggravated. She quickly took a seat. The wolf wanted out. Even in her dream, she had no peace.

"You should just leave, go on with what you were planning and forget me. It is what I would do. Just leave my troubles behind, friends and family. Leave them all behind to live another day. You are not ready for what is going to happen, for what you are going to become."

Emily knew the voice. Ashley appeared from the darkness. Her hair was tied back in a ponytail, and she wore a white shirt half-covered by a sweater and cargo pants. Emily could not see her feet, twisted underneath her.

"I understand…go and don't look back, there is no sense in both of us dying at the hands of this creep."

"He will not stop with you…" Emily continued to have a hard time sitting straight. Her eyes blurred to the point nothing was clear to her but Ashley. "He knew you were the only one I would not leave behind."

"I care nothing about you. I only wanted to get in your pants, dear Emily. It was all about sex, a teenage crush. I could never let go."

"You lie," Emily quickly stated.

"Don't be stupid. Just leave me. Leave everything—all these people, put as much distance between you and this monster as you can. Maybe you can settle down somewhere and live out your life and he will never find you."

"You are wrong, Ash. He is not the monster—not the only one anyways. I am like him. I taste it in my own blood, and I crave it now. I will be just like him."

"I know you, the only sister I claimed. My family abandoned me because of who I am. Your father hates me because I'm gay. Always thought I was a bad influence on you. You have done more for me than anyone I have ever known and I want you to leave. Put it all behind you. You are not like him, and I would never forgive myself, or you, for coming back for me."

"Your blood will be on my hands if I leave, and I will never forgive myself. I might as well die because I cannot live with that," she proclaimed.

"She is right, you know. You are a monster."

Emily looked to her left and seated next to her was Detective Vance, throat ripped open, chest cavity exposed where her heart once beat.

"*You are exactly like him and should be put down like the bitch dog you are.*"

"I am sorry."

"*Your words mean nothing, look at what you did to me,*" Vance replied.

"*She may have killed you, but trust the opinion of an old man, this little lady is nothing like the other.*"

Emily looked up seeing the figure of old Mathew Bradley standing behind Ashley.

"*I am glad I was there that night to save you. You have to believe your little friend here.*" The old man looked down, smiling at Ashley and placing his hand on her shoulder. Ashley returned a big smile back at the old man before they both looked back at her. "*Believe me, you were willing to leave your friends behind and lead him away from here to protect them. Not just from him but also from your own fear of killing someone you love. That act alone should make you believe you are nothing like him.*"

"*…I did not deserve to die like that,*" Vance yelled staring at Emily. "*Not like this, my body still rotting in some vacant barn—who knows when I will be found…or if I ever will be found. I'll just melt away…*"

"I am sorry," Emily said

"*An apology is not enough.*"

"*She is right, you know. An apology is not enough.*"

Another familiar voice joined the group. She looked to see Colin walking through the darkness.

"*You will have to make it right by her, what you did.*"

Vance disappeared as Colin approached sitting down beside Ashley.

"*Sometime, down the road, you will have to make amends for what you did, but you must believe you are good enough to do what has to be done. You must believe in yourself, you are enough to kill the other one. This is not just about you and your circle of friends and family. When he is done with them, he is only going to start a new hunt, —kill more people, and maybe even infect someone else.*"

"Always the Boy Scout. I never did like you and your country good boy routine." Troy Anders came from her left standing for only a moment before he took a seat close to Emily. *"You fucked him, and then you dreamed about killing him. I always knew there was something between the two of you, even though you denied it. Same goes with that little dyke."* Troy motioned toward Ashley who had twisted her head to one side, it was then Emily realized the old man was gone. *"Little slut, you were moments from fucking the bell boy too, the guy from the club, even the bastard who did this to me."* Troy turned his head to show her the left side of his face and throat, both were shredded cartilage, bone, and blood.

"She never loved you, you have no business here," Ashley said in the harshest of tone. The figure got up from her seated position, walking around the pit, and sat down directly next to Emily. She knew it was not real, but she could almost feel the woman's touch on her hand.

"You are wrong Ashley. I know you all hated him, but some part of me did love him…and like so many others, he did not deserve to die this way," Emily called out. The look of sadness in her friend's eyes sent a chill up her back. "I did hate you in the end… even if I almost gave into you that night. It would have been a mistake." She could almost feel the tight grip of Ashley's hand on hers. "And I have made mistakes, close calls since the attack…but you have no right…" She looked to Colin and then back to Troy who was gone. "You two…and my parents are the most important people in my life." She glanced from Ashley to Colin, and she then saw her parents embracing each other behind him. They gave her a knowing smile before they, and Colin, disappeared.

Emily felt the touch of Ashley's head on her shoulder. *"And then it was just the two of us. How did we end up here?"*

"You have to know, I am coming for you. I will not let him kill you." Emily said with a smile, squeezing her hand harder.

"I will be waiting…"

She felt the touch of her hand and head only for another moment before she was gone, and she sat all alone in the tent.

"You mean I will not let him kill her."

Emily looked across the steam to see the other woman. It was *her*. Naked and soaked in blood, it was the same vision she had of herself the last night she stayed in the hospital.

"I am inside you; we are one and the same. You only have to let me out to do what must be done. The only way you can save your friend and kill him is to let me out. Let me run wild." The other Emily smiled a big smile. She lifted her bloody hand and licked the side as she kept an eye on the other Emily, *"The taste of human blood is almost indescribable… the texture is so rich and sweet by comparison to other. You will have to embrace me to get through this…"*

"NO!" EMILY SCREAMED. She glanced at the clock knowing it was only a matter of time before the morning alarm sounded. She sat up, the thick comforter fell to her waist..She could feel it against her bare legs. She did not remember much after Hastings left. She glanced at her phone to see two missed calls, both from Colin.

Emily glanced at the cracked-open door and the darkness beyond. She shifted her legs over the edge of the bed, crossing to the bathroom. She sat on the edge of the tub turning the water on and felt the hot liquid as it ran over her hand, before reaching down and plugging the tub. She stood and looked in the mirror. She could see the steam from the tub as it floated into the room, and it reminded her of the dream. The last thing she remembered was talking to her…her other self. She splashed warm water on her face and stared into her own eyes. A wicked smile graced her lips, one of lust and hunger—the same smile her other always expressed. But, it was not the other staring back at her now. She turned from her reflection, undressing and stepping into the tub. Emily slowly slid down letting the water wash over her.

There was no noise, she saw him step into the room with her cell phone in hand. "You're getting bad about breaking in."

"You need to start locking your door," he replied. Colin was dressed in mostly camouflage.

"He hasn't called yet. He's waiting for dark; he wants it to be dark or as close to sundown as possible, before he will arrange the meeting."

"He thinks he has the advantage." Colin leaned against the doorway. "You want some company?" he questioned, with a large smile.

"I need to save my aggression for…something else." She returned the smile. "Besides, last time we got intimate I nearly exposed your heart." She raised her hands from the water to show her fingers to him. "He knows I won't come alone. Even though I may be afraid of killing others, he knows you will be with me." Emily took a long deep breath. "Promise me something."

"Anything."

"Promise me when it starts you will get Ashley out of there. Don't worry about killing Devon, or me, you get her out of wherever he is keeping her," Emily stated, her hand disappeared back under the water.

"I promise," Colin replied, turning to leave the room.

Emily closed her eyes, drifting, enjoying the warm water for another moment.

———•———

EMILY SAT OUTSIDE, leaning forward in her chair. Most of the day had passed and still no call. She could hear Colin in the other room, but was in no hurry to join him. She wore loose-fitting jeans—already ripped-up at purchase and a warm, black V-neck top. Fuzzy boots stretched just below her knees—she could never remember wearing them before today. Her hair was pulled back in a ponytail, though loose strands of red still covered her face. No make-up or jewelry. She held the cold coffee cup in one hand, and phone in the other.

"You have any sort of plan Emily?"

She looked up to see Colin standing in the doorway. "I am the plan. I've made him bleed once…he wants revenge. You will hold back until I can get him away from Ashley and then get her to safety."

An intense, cold wind sent a chill down her back; she could smell the rain in the air. "He will be calling anytime." Emily looked back at Colin. "If this turns bad…you may have to do something neither of us has addressed."

"And we're not going to now either," he quickly replied.

"It's going to rain tonight…maybe even snow—" The phone beeped breaking her from what she was about to say. A text message from Ashley's phone: *Mathew Bradley's cabin.*

She looked toward him. "He is waiting at Mathew Bradley's cabin."

"Let's go," he stated.

"Ten minutes, Colin–give me a ten-minute head start."

Emily rushed out into the yard. It was then Colin came after her, but by the time they reached her jeep, she had the engine going and was starting to back away. She stopped when Colin reached the door, rolling down the window they gave each other a smile as he leaned in slowly kissing her lips. No other words were said as she backed out of the drive.

⬤

EMILY WASTED NO time getting to Bradley's cabin. As she approached the gate, she revved the engine. It was locked. She pulled the jeep into gear and crashed through the gate. On impact the jeep lurched momentarily sideways, the front spinning into the ditch.

She pulled it into reverse and after a few spins, backed up, pulled it into gear again, and started up the road toward the Bradley cabin. She stopped at the sign she remembered seeing the first time they were here, and thought about the conversation with Bradley. The night everything changed—when she knew what had truly happened to her.

Her phone blasted for the fifth time in the last thirty minutes, and she knew it was Colin before she even glared at the name. She tossed it to the seat beside her. He was likely less than ten minutes behind her. Even though she was heavy footed on the drive here, she knew Colin would have done the same. She released the brake allowing the jeep to move up and around the curve. She could see the cabin now, smoke billowed from the chimney. It was close to dark, she could feel it, the wolf would come out tonight.

Emily came to a stop right at the edge of the drive, pulling the jeep into gear and shutting the engine off. She sat there for a couple of minutes and quickly sent a text message, before she opened the door stepping outside. Hidden from anyone who watched from the cabin, she pulled the pistol from the top of one of her bags and put it in the waistband of her jeans leaving the holster in the seat. She backed away from the door letting it close gently. She could smell him.

She slowly approached the door. She was several yards away when it opened. The light from the cabin spilled out into the yard. A glance at the sky above the sun was nearly tipping the distant tree line.

"I was beginning to wonder if you were going to make it in time. I was itching for a little snack." Devon grinned.

He wore no shirt, and for the first time, she could see he was ripped—thick chest and arms, held by a thick muscular abdomen. Every muscle seemed to shine in the dim light. He held something in his mouth, but from the distance she couldn't tell what. He wore ripped-up, old jeans with the button undone, and she could not take her eyes from the muscles disappearing into the cloth.

"We were worried you may actually try to run again. We have a party inside—why don't you come and join us?" He turned, stepping back into the cabin and disappeared from view.

Emily stepped up into the cabin and was not prepared to see what she did. The first person she saw was Kari. Bound to a chair with a gag in her mouth, she wore similar clothing to the last time she saw her. It was possible Devon had even taken her that day.

"Oh, I see—you did not expect to see such an audience for the festivities." Devon, who had taken a position behind Kari, pointed off into the small kitchen area. "Ladies, the guest of honor is here!"

Ashley was bound, gagged, and looked unconscious–tied in a corner. Even from the distance, she could see her arms were bruised and cut up.

"You bastard."

"She is alive," Devon smiled. He circled around to the other end of the table.

Emily could see a third person behind him—tied up much the same as Kari and Ashley—but could not tell who it was.

"Please, have a seat." He motioned to the chair across from him. "We have…" He looked at his watch, "…around fifteen to twenty minutes to catch up." He grinned taking a seat and propping his bare feet up on the table. "I must say, I am surprised you came alone, I figured little blond Boy Scout would be at your side—but I am guessing he is not far behind."

"Let them go. I am here. They don't have to be here." Emily approached the chair, but did not sit.

"Please, you and I both know this is the way it has to be." He sneered. "It all comes down to you, Ms. Meyer. You and I are one and the same—killers, monsters. I have to say, I underestimated you the other night, and you gave me a nasty scar for it." He leaned his head to one side showing the still red welt from where she had bitten him. "But it felt good too–a challenge even. And, I believe you have a kill on you since then. You think you can control the beast, enough so you can kill me and not those you love. You are still no match for me, and after tonight I will move on—but not without one good slaughter." He ran a hand under Kari's chin. She tried to pull away but he held a firm grip.

"You are a sick, twisted son of a bitch," Emily stated.

Devon quit moving his hand on the other woman's skin to glare at her "Maybe. I wish I could say it was the wolf who did all of those killings, Emily, but I had an infatuation with death before." He crossed his arms against his chest. "Five murders before the faithful night I picked the wrong victim," he stated. "She was a lot like you, fought against her natural instinct to hunt. She looked like a librarian—which was my… taste. Simple girl next door types, lady in the street and a freak in the bedroom. They were so easy to charm—even her. She fell for every word I said and I got her back to my motel."

"So you were a sick fuck even before you got infected—no surprise there—not enough love from mommy, or just couldn't get it up?" Emily's voice grew harsher with each word.

"It is rude to interrupt my story. Now, let me continue. I got her on her back; tied to the bed—the moment the rope went on she started struggling. I knew then there was something different about her. The others liked a little kink in it. But, not her—everything about her changed when she was tied up, and I thought helpless. She quit struggling when I pulled the knife. That was my first warning. That is when she started to laugh at me. The opposite of the first four—they started begging and whimpering—but she only laughed. It pissed me off. Why would she laugh at me when I was so evidently going to kill her? That is when she started to change, her voice, and her eyes, everything about her started to change. I don't know when, but at some point, I knew I wasn't the only killer in that room. Or the deadliest…"

"Very similar to your current situation," Emily said with a big smile. She wanted to wink or even clap for him but her hand sat on her hips slowly inching toward her back.

"Funny girl," Devon said, with an understanding smile. "She broke free, attacked me, and left me these four pretty little scars." He pointed to the ones on his left shoulder. "I guess they may be a lot like the ones on your own shoulder. She left me alive though—something I don't intend on doing for you." Devon began to unlatch his watch and set it on the table.

Emily did not have to know the time, she felt it deep down, and it grew even more unpleasant as she watched him stand and smile.

"It is time," Devon said, placing his hands on the table and arching his neck forward.

"Yes, I suppose…" Emily quickly pulled the pistol from her back pocket—and before he could move—shot twice, not knowing how well she hit him as he fell away from her. "I really hope that killed you."

She circled around and started to untie Kari. As Emily fought with the knot, she fell to one side on the floor. The growing pain was too great. With hazy eyes, she glanced at the floor on the other side of the table. Devon was on all fours, in the middle of his transformation as well.

EMILY WISHED SHE had more control. To speed up her own transformation, it was an advantage she knew she didn't have. A fierce rumble of—twisting, turning, and thrashing—bodies hitting the floor roughly. Emily stopped, lying on her side. She could see every twitch and turn of the man she had hoped she had killed. He was not in as much pain as she was. She could tell he was even enjoying his transformation. All she wanted to do was scream out in horror.

Emily could see Kari's tied hands as the other woman struggled to break free with no success. Still seizing, Emily glanced at her now sharp nails, stretching to reach and with a quick swipe of her hand cut through the ropes on the woman's wrists.

"Free others," Emily mumbled, rolling over onto her hands and knees. Her neck arched, she could feel the teeth in her mouth enlarging and her jaw dislocating—making room for the sharp razor-like teeth. Piercing nails dug and scratched at the seasoned wood. She glanced toward the door, just in time to see the woman she had just freed run into the darkness, not waiting around to help the others. Emily's body ached and arched unnaturally into the air as she came to rest on her knees. The pain was intense. She studied her hands and wrists as they grew leaner, longer, and more muscular. She tried to scream out in pain, but only a growl-mixed-howl escaped. She could hear him even though he was out of sight now, his deep growling-laugh at her pain.

Emily stood, like her hands, the rest of her body grew in size as her shirt began to shred under the pressure, as did the rest of her clothing. She released a long, loud growl of pain as she stumbled backward into the table. Emily fell to the floor. In the door she glanced and could see the terror in Ashley's eyes. She heard Devon stalking behind her. Emily crawled out the door, still her body changing, she struggled, pulling herself forward trying to lure him away. She wanted to speak, his shadow lingering over her from the light of the cabin. Emily reached the edge of the light from the door and his shadow melted with the darkness. She turned, pushing away on her back, and even in her current state, she wanted to scream when she saw him.

The werewolf approached, dark brown fur—the same shade as Devon's hair—covered his body. She could still see the features of a man's face even though the muzzle of a wolf glared at her. His arms—covered in short dark hair—were longer and more muscular than before. He flexed his massive hands as he looked at her. He stalked her, much like he did the night of the attack. She could see his eyes—the same color as before but with a hint of yellow—and his teeth…long and sharp as he smiled. Drool seeped from his mouth as his teeth gleamed and sparkled on exposure.

"It is time, little bitch." His voice was hoarse and each word was cut with a shrill hint of a growl. "Time to finish what I started." He towered over her ready to strike with an upraised claw.

Emily scooted away from him, pushing her weight in the dirt. Her body still fought against every movement, not prepared for the change. She could feel every shift inside her own body. She grew stronger with each second. She felt the tingle of hairs as they grew where there were none before—as red as crimson, they hid the once human flesh. Her face shifted and morphed into something more animal than human and her eyes locked on the eyes of the beast still following her. But, through it all…she knew who she was. The other only laughed, watching her stumble to her feet and weave off toward the wilderness.

"You cannot hide from me," he called out with an intense growl. A long, eerie howl followed. "Come out, come out wherever you are."

Emily could hear the animals scatter as she approached. She fell into the soft mud in an attempt to catch her breath. The pain had subsided, but she only wanted to run—to get away from the one chasing her, something she was unable to do that night. She took two deep breaths before she again stumbled to her feet. Taking three steps forward, she heard him…there in the clearing with her. It was too dark and she could see nothing moving—even with her advanced vision.

"My, oh my, what big teeth you have," he said, landing in a crouching position his head leaning to one side. She did the same as she scowled at him turning to get a better look, as he kneeled several feet away. Emily took a moment, raised her hands looking at the unfamiliar claws; they were more grotesque than she had seen in her previous transformations, her fingers longer and more muscular supporting thicker claws. She looked up just as he leaped, but he jumped past her and ran through the darkness.

A long-winded growl escaped Emily. She knew she should go the other direction, but there was something else going on inside her. She wanted to pursue him. To kill him. She turned and ran after him, limbs smacked at her face, but she had no problem dodging them. She could hear him several yards away still in a full run. And then…nothing. She slowed her pace to a stalk. Emily moved, watching with each step she took, hoping to see him. She could smell him, but could not place where he was.

The laugh brought her to an instant stop twisting to look back at him, positioned against the tree he watched every move she made.

"Do you really think you have what it takes to kill me?"

Emily growled in reply. She faced him ready to leap, to attack.

"I don't think you do pup."

A long fierce roar escaped Emily as she leaped. Devon swiped across her face leaving four long gashes across her cheek. Blood immediately poured to the ground as she pushed up from the mud, but she did not feel the pain. She only growled.

"You can do better than that, I know it." He laughed.

Emily stood, blood matted in her fur as she took a deep breath and slowly approached.

"Show me you were worthy of our gift." Full of confidence, he took a small step toward her.

Emily swung wildly and repeatedly, but Devon avoided each attack. The fourth time, he caught both her wrists. He snarled and swung her—tossing her away, not giving her a chance to bite.

"Fool me once." He laughed, approaching, just as she started to stand. Devon took a big handful of hair, running his fingernails from his free hand up her back, cutting into flesh. He pushed her forward, releasing the grip, as she turned watching him lick the blood from his fingers. "Like strawberries," he said. "Too sweet for me to share."

"Our gift? Share?" Emily ran a hand across the wound on her cheek. "You're not alone…"

"So many bodies in my path. I don't think I ever claimed to be the only one here hunting." Devon continued to look at the blood on his hands. "She wanted you for herself—bitch on bitch. It is the only reason I didn't kill you that night at your home. I am going to take great pleasure in gutting you." He approached.

Emily looked back at him. When he was in reach she did not attack with her hands, but lunged with mouth open. Teeth ripped through his throat as claws dug into his stomach. She tore with her mouth and hands. She felt his hands on her, trying to push her off, but she was latched on, ripping through muscle. She released and he fell to the ground, almost immediately he began to shift back to his human form.

He coughed blood, trying to speak as she reached out with one last swipe.

"No last words," she said, looking off in the direction they had come knowing there was another wolf.

EMILY STEPPED FROM the forest. She could feel the wound throbbing on her back even though he had barely broken the skin. It hurt more than the marks on her face. It had seemed like an hour to her, but only a matter of minutes had actually passed. She watched as Colin bolted from his vehicle, rushing into the cabin. She could hear the rumble from the inside, even" from where she stood. Her heart beat up into her throat. Emily had known who the other wolf was the moment she started back through the forest.

Colin came from the cabin with two women, one on each arm—all heading toward his truck. She could see the other woman clearer now, she had never gotten a good enough look before as she had spent her time concentrating on Devon, it was Lauren.

Lauren stopped while Colin attended to Ashley. She could hear Colin ask, "Has anyone seen Emily or the old man?"

"I saw her…" said Ashley. Ashley's complexion was pale, she was in shock.

"The old man is dead. I saw the other guy kill him," Lauren replied.

Emily inched closer. She didn't want to cause a reaction from the other werewolf, but also needed a moment to gather her own strength. She could see something moving in the background behind them. Kari appeared, walking into the light beside Lauren. The woman was out of breath; Emily could see it easily as-she collapsed to her knees.

"Where is Emily?" Colin questioned, walking frantically back-and-forth.

"She…he…" Kari stuttered. She pointed off in Emily's direction. "That way." They all looked but she was sure only Lauren saw her. Lauren smiled. She circled around stepping between them.

"She is there." Lauren grinned. Her hand cut through Kari's throat in an instant, and she was behind Colin just as fast—knocking the gun from his hand. She held a hand full of his hair with her free hand. "Come on out, Emily."

Ashley was frozen in shock unable to move.

"The girl next door…the fifth victim," Emily growled, stepping into the light, still in her werewolf state and covered in blood.

"Yes, he told you the story of how he was turned. I warned him not to underestimate you." Lauren held Colin tight against her. Her long nails dug into the soft skin of his throat until they pierced the flesh. Blood ran down until it disappeared into his shirt under the grasp on her arm keeping Colin pulled against her. The only thing Emily could see of the woman was her different hair; the streaked blond seemed to shine in the moonlight.

"Please, just let him go," Ashley called out.

"Sorry, lover, I plan on saving you for last. I had wanted one more hour of passion with you, but alas, it is not to be. Maybe I'll have fun with your corpse."

"Why didn't you just kill me…in the hospital you had your chance?" Emily backed away, partially hidden by the darkness.

"It crossed my mind, dear. All I had to do was turn off the monitors and reopen your wounds. It would have just looked like shitty work by the hick surgeons." She repositioned Colin so she could look at Emily. "The wolf got the better of me, I guess. The idea of being a pack mother interested me. Of course, I did not realize how quickly you would mature or how hard it would be to take you from your friends. So grounded in your life here. I thought maybe killing your boyfriend would push you over the edge…didn't realize he was a bastard you wanted nothing to do with."

"Bad representation…Devon was so easy to hate." Emily paced back-and-forth hardly able to control her urge to attack.

"A month I made him wait to kill the Erma wolf—let me get settled into my new identity—and what did he do? Five people in one night…and let one live, and a sixth see him…the fool," Lauren stated. "For him, it was all about the blood, the kill, and not the hunt. I should have never let him turn—should have torn him to pieces the night in the hotel and went about my way of life. But something inside wanted a change…"

"The wolf wanted out." Emily continued to pace and growl.

"Yes, it did. It was tired of being chained to a tree twice a month and not let run, roam. It is an animal within us, after all. We are not meant to be tied down, it is not natural," Lauren stated.

Their eyes stayed glued to one another despite Emily's pacing.

Lauren was still in human form only her eyes and long nails showed different. "I'm nearly fifty. I have lived and done so much in my life." She glanced at Ashley, who had a look of disbelief on her face. "Not a day over thirty, I know, lover. Emily can thank you as well, that first night in the hospital I had gotten everyone out of the room but you. I wasn't even supposed to be there that night, the fool let Emily live and I just beat the old man to the emergency room. For the better part of the night, I waited patiently for nurses and doctors to leave her side and just as they did….Ashley arrived and stayed right there with her hand in yours. I paced back-and-forth in front of the door hoping you would grow tired and leave, but you were persistent lover. And loyal, like a good little puppy."

"I will never be like you," Ashley called out.

"We will have to see how this plays out. I assume you made sure Devon was dead before you came back here…and you already knew there was another or you would have probably left," Lauren stated. Colin struggled to stand and the grimace of pain on his face from her nails in his neck was growing more obvious.

"I ripped the bastard's throat and heart out—he will not be coming back to you."

"Pity, but you saved me the trouble. Tonight would have been our last night as mates." Lauren smiled. "They say wolves mate for life, Devon's death frees me to take another." Lauren twisted to look at Ashley.

"Never going to happen, bitch," Ashley replied, finally finding enough composure to stand.

"Such hurtful words." She twisted to look at Colin. "How about you Blondie? You looking for a fun, exciting sexual experience?" She leaned forward and ran her tongue across Colin's ear while winking at Emily. "And I bet you haven't told her…you feel the wolf inside you. Those wounds on your chest given in the heat of passion? You are already one of us."

Colin's eyes met Emily's for only a moment.

"Sorry, been there done that would rather keep to my own…" he said, with a spry smile.

"Guess that leaves you and me, Red," Lauren said with a smile. Her nails dug into Colin's throat farther and she pulled before anyone could move. He fell to the ground holding his neck. Lauren leaped at Ashley knocking the woman back to the ground.

Emily saw her claws raise, she was already in motion pushing Lauren away before she could strike. She did not stop her progress until they slammed hard into the truck. The truck moved under the hit, sliding sideways, pushing Ashley toward them as they collapsed beside her.

Lauren pinned Emily to the ground even though Lauren wasn't fully transformed Emily could not over power her. She glared at Ashley, "Look, the threesome I am sure you wanted." Lauren stretched her body out toward Ashley but she quickly backed away and into the truck.

"Not her, this is between you and me." Emily pushed the woman with her knees until she released her grip.

Gunshots rang out. Colin gripped the gun with one hand and his bleeding throat with the other. Lauren leaped off heading toward him.

Emily flinched when she felt the touch of another—Ashley on her knees, a hand on her shoulder. As their eyes met, she pulled her hand away. "You have to get up," Ashley muttered, showing no fear of what her friend had become—but sorrow shadowed her eyes as she again placed a hand on her shoulder. "I think I need you to break up with my girlfriend for me." A smile graced her lips—one shared by Emily even in wolf form. She was still her best friend.

Emily turned away from her friend, pushing her weight from the ground, and growled. She was even more surprised as her friend helped her get steady. They exchanged another glance of friendship before she looked to see Lauren standing over Colin. It was obvious by her blood-soaked hands; she had finished what she'd started. Emily leaped. She landed near Lauren and struck—slicing her face, before she could grab her wrist throwing her to the ground.

"You have lost a lot of blood, almost not fair." Lauren grabbed her wrists, holding her against the ground. She pulled them together to hold them with only one hand. Her right hand now free, she placed it at Emily's chin turning it to one side. She lowered and ran her tongue up her face, and then bit her own lip. "It is not too late you know. We can go away just the two of us…or even the three of us." She glanced at Ashley who was now hovering over Colin. "I know it must be a tempting offer." She lifted away from Emily, releasing her grip on her face.

Emily lifted her head, exposing her teeth—growling and snarling as she tried to bite.

"So cute." Lauren laughed at Emily's intimidation attempt.

It had taken Lauren's attention off Ashley. Two gunshots echoed, both striking Lauren in the chest and knocking her off Emily.

Emily rolled over on her stomach, she was growing weak—feeling herself almost about to shift back to her human form. She twisted her head to look at Lauren, who was in a similar position and in midst of her shift. Emily stumbled to her feet away from where Lauren kneeled.

Before Emily could capitalize on her wounded prey, she moved, Lauren was on her snarling and growling faster than anything she had ever seen.

"It was a nice try." Her fingers tightly around Emily throat, she growled and tossed her back into Ashley. Lauren looked at the wounds inflicted by the bullets and snarled before charging on all fours toward them.

Emily rolled out of the way as Ashley aimed and shot, again and again and again, until only the clicking of an empty gun rang out. "I don't think things are going to work out between us."

Emily rolled to face their attacker. Lauren—now on her knees several feet away—had stopped moving. Emily leaped, hitting the woman in the chest. Rolling over and over, they continued snapping at each other-until Emily's teeth dug into her shoulder. A harsh howl escaped the more experienced wolf and she shook violently. Emily growled, releasing her grip, claws digging into the other wolf's arms, pushing her away from her friend and into the darkness. They both rushed at each other again, equally landing slashes and bites as they tangled and rolled across the ground—leaving a trail of blood through the mud.

"Crazy bitch." Lauren circled around her sideways on all fours. "You should've left after you killed Devon." She snarled and growled.

Emily, lifted herself barely off the ground, blood pouring from countless wounds looked at her before she wobbled and fell to the ground. "And let you kill Ashley?" She spat excess fluid from her mouth; more blood than saliva. "I am sorry to disappoint you…but you should be used to it with a protégé like Devon."

Emily rose up to her knees, looking at the other wolf—dark patches of blood caked to fur and flesh. Lauren snarled. She also recognized her wounds as she rose to a similar position, resting on her knees. Both women had reverted to lesser wolf shifts, only a hint on their face and hands still evident.

Lauren placed her hand on the bite on her shoulder and pulled it free to see it covered in red crimson, then to her other hand as she removed it from her stomach to the dark-red blood. The wound on her stomach was fatal. "You crazy, fucking bitch."

Emily held her side, but she had a hard time holding her composure as she stood and approached. She stopped just out of arms reach. "I will not be like you. I will never let the wolf control me."

Lauren laughed looking up at her, the feral in her eyes gone. "Thirty years I told myself I was in control, until I let it out just the once…since then I no longer had my humanity. I was only the wolf." She launched her body toward Emily from her knees.

On reflex, Emily's long fingers slashed leaving four deep gashes across Lauren's face—cutting into flesh and bone. She was dead before she hit the ground.

Emily collapsed to her knees and immediately started to cry. Head in hands, she heard the crack of a limb. She breathed a sigh of relief when she saw Ashley there. Ashley had a similar look of relief.

"Are you okay?" Ashley questioned.

Emily started to laugh as she sat back on her legs and turned to look at the mauled corpse of Lauren at her side.

"I don't know," she replied.

"You have lost a lot of blood." Ashley pushed the gun into the top of her pants and took off her shirt as she approached. "We need to get you to a hospital."

"I need to leave here," Emily stated, letting her friend help her up the path.

They got back to the vehicles.

"Don't look."

Emily could see Colin's cold eyes staring at her and she began to cry, pulling away from Ashley. She hobbled over to her friend and she fell to her knees, pulling his head to her lap. "I'm so sorry." She lowered her head, kissing him on the forehead. Her tears were flowing nonstop now.

Emily felt Ashley's hand on her shoulder, she glanced back to see her friend crying. She could never remember seeing Ashley cry—not even at her father's funeral.

"I need to get you to a hospital."

"No…"

THE LAST THING Emily remembered was Ashley helping her into her jeep—and Colin, his once warm eyes staring at her…cold and empty. She rolled over with little realization of where she was. This was not a hospital. She knew she should be hurting but wasn't. She could feel the bandages on her face and most of her upper body. Emily sat up slowly, she was stiff, but still no pain. She saw Ashley immediately—on the floor in the corner covered up and asleep.

"Nice to see you awake."

She shifted to see Max Erma standing in the door. She remembered now, the text she had sent before she confronted Devon. It was her escape.

"The firecracker has barely left your side, nursed you back to health."

"How long have I been out?"

"Three weeks," the man stated. "You are lucky. I have a friend with some medical training and no ethics. He patched you up, gave you the medicine and a blood transfusion without any questions or I'm sure you'd not be breathing right now. You lost a lot of blood."

"I don't feel it…"

"The wolf is healing you," he replied. "Your friend said you killed them both. So, there were two of them."

"A man and woman," she answered.

"Thank you for avenging my brother," he said, turning to leave the room.

Emily throwing the covers off. She crossed the room wearing only a long shirt. Kneeling down, she placed her hand on Ashley's forehead. Her friend opened her eyes.

"You're awake."

"Thanks to you," she stated.

Ashley shifted to a sitting position. "I still believe we should have gone to a hospital."

"And explained my injuries how?—or the stuff at the cabin…" She couldn't hide the sorrow on her face.

"I went to his funeral. Your parents were there. A Detective Hastings too. He was there looking for you," Ashley stated. "I told them I hadn't seen you since the day before Colin was found. He thinks you—he knows—there is something different about you. They found his partner…"

"I have to leave here—run." Emily said, as she stood.

"I am going with you." Ashley pulled herself to her feet.

"No." Emily walked to the bed. She could see her bags on the opposite side of the room. "They could track my jeep,"

"Miles, miles away from here—as well as your cell phone, if they were to find it…they wouldn't know to look here," Ashley replied. "I am coming with you."

Emily turned. Her friend was right beside her now. "No. I need you to stay; I need you to look after my family. Maybe one day I can return home…but I have to put as much distance between the people I love and the wolf as I can," Emily leaned forward kissing Ashley on the forehead.

EPILOGUE

I'VE LOST TRACK *of time…I don't know how long it's been since I was bitten, let alone when I left home. Maybe that is why I've started this journal…. It's been at least a month, maybe two since I left. I wish I could say I had control but spring is almost here and I haven't let the wolf out since…. since…. It wants out nightly. It's getting harder to keep it at bay and I've been blacking out. I have a feeling I will turn tonight…I pray the chains hold me…*

About the Author

Born and raised in the hills of eastern Kentucky, Steven Paul Watson is many things: a writer, artist, amateur photographer, and avid outdoorsman as well as an all-around geek.

His love of writing includes soul-chilling science fiction, fantasy, and all things supernatural/horror. But his true passion is steampunk/alternate reality.

Attending more than a handful of conventions a year, he stays close to his geeky roots. When out in nature, Steven enjoys running multiple 5Ks a year and hiking the hills near his home.

www.ingramcontent.com/pod-product-compliance
Lightning Source LLC
Chambersburg PA
CBHW060551190726

48283CB00003B/959